The Real People
Book One

THE WAY OF THE PRIESTS

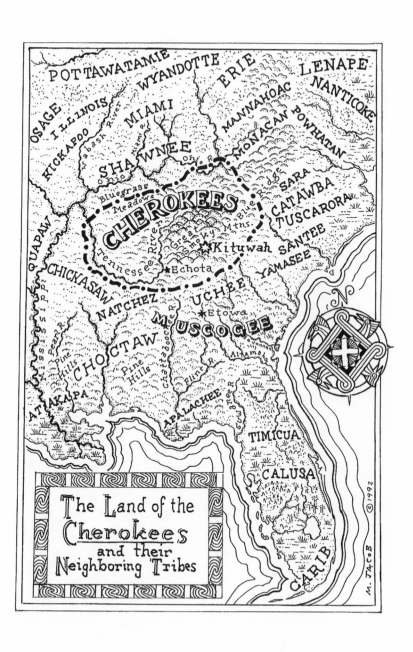

POTTAWATAMIE
WYANDOTTE
ERIE
LENAPE
NANTICOKE
OSAGE
ILLINOIS
KICKAPOO
Wabash River
MIAMI
MANNAHOAC
MONACAN
POWHATAN
SHAWNEE
Ohio
Blue Ridge
SARA
CATAWBA
TUSCARORA
Bluegrass Meadows
CHEROKEES
Great Smoky Mtns.
Kituwah
SANTEE
QUAPAW
Tennessee River
Echota
YAMASEE
CHICKASAW
NATCHEZ
UCHEE
Etowa
Mississippi R.
Pearl R.
Pine Hills
CHOCTAW
Pine Hills
Chattahoochee R.
MUSCOGEE
Flint R.
Alabama
Suwanee R.
ATAKAPA
APALACHEE
TIMICUA
CALUSA
N

The Land of the
Cherokees
and their
Neighboring Tribes

CARIB

© 1992

M. JACOB

Also by Robert J. Conley

Back to Malachi
The Actor
The Witch of Goingsnake and Other Stories
Wilder and Wilder
Killing Time
Colfax
Quitting Time
The Saga of Henry Starr
Ned Christie's War
Nickajack

ROBERT J. CONLEY

The Way

of the Priests

A Double D Western

D O U B L E D A Y

New York   London   Toronto   Sydney   Auckland

A Double D Western
PUBLISHED BY DOUBLEDAY
a division of Bantam Doubleday Dell Publishing Group, Inc.
666 Fifth Avenue, New York, New York 10103

Double D Western, Doubleday,
and the portrayal of the letters DD
are trademarks of Doubleday, a division of
Bantam Doubleday Dell Publishing Group, Inc.

Map and illustrations by Murv Jacob

Library of Congress Cataloging-in-Publication Data

Conley, Robert J.
The way of the priests/Robert J. Conley.—1st ed.
  p.   cm.—(The Real people; bk. 1) (A Double D western)
1. Cherokee Indians—Fiction. I. Title. II. Series.
PS3553.O494W3   1992
813'.54—dc20   92-10142
CIP

ISBN 0-385-41932-5
Copyright © 1992 by Robert J. Conley
All Rights Reserved
Printed in the United States of America
November 1992
First Edition

10 9 8 7 6 5 4 3 2 1

15.00

For all of the Real People

THE WAY OF THE PRIESTS

One

SALOLI, THE GRAY SQUIRREL, must have heard the approach of the children, for he stopped his chattering and sat still on the oak tree branch. He was watching, a picture of total caution. On the ground, maybe thirty paces away, the three children stopped. They were big children, of an age when their childhood was almost over. They would not be children much longer, and probably they knew that, and that knowledge made them play all the more and all the harder at being children while they were still able. Of course they looked forward with eagerness to the responsibilities and the respect of adulthood, to the imagined pleasures of maturity, but they were at the ambiguous time of life when the forward-looking eagerness was balanced with a tenacious clinging to the joys of childish irresponsibility.

The one in the lead was a girl, *agehyuja*. Her name was Selu Ajiluhsgi, or Corn Flower, and she was not only physically ahead of the two boys, her companions, but she was also clearly the leader of the trio. It was she who had seen the squirrel, had signaled a halt to the march and had called for silence. Two paces behind and to her right, Tsis-quaya, Real Bird or Sparrow, watched with unconcealed admiration as Corn Flower slipped a thistledown tufted honey locust dart into one end of her long cane pole blowgun. Already one squirrel had fallen to her deadly aim, and it was hanging limp from a cord around her waist. Sparrow had two, and the third member of the party, Gule, Acorn, standing on a line with Sparrow but to Corn Flower's left, had one.

As Corn Flower slowly raised the gun toward her lips, Sparrow saw out of the corner of his eye Acorn quickly load his own gun and take a too fast shot. The squirrel screamed out in anger, surprise and pain as the sharp dart buried itself in his thigh. He jumped and twisted on the branch, biting at the dart, and then Corn Flower fired a clean shot to the head, and the squirrel dropped.

"Good shot," said Sparrow. He ran toward the prize only a stride behind Corn Flower. Acorn sauntered along at a pouty pace.

"Now everyone but me has two," he said. His chin was practically on his chest, and his lower lip protruded. Sparrow glanced back and noticed how Acorn's hips were swinging heavily from side to side as he walked. He had only recently observed his friend's effeminate characteristics, and he was worried about him. One day he had gone home after play, and he had told his mother.

"Gule acts like a girl sometimes," he had said.

Gatuhnlati, Wild Hemp, his mother, had looked thoughtful for a moment before answering.

"I hadn't thought about it before," she had said, "but since you mentioned it, I guess I have noticed. He has no father, you know, and even worse, his mother has no brothers, only sisters. He's been around women and girls most of his life. I guess he doesn't know how else to act."

"He plays with me," Sparrow had said, "and I don't act like that."

"Of course you don't," she had said, "but the biggest influence is at home."

So Sparrow had decided to spend as much time with Acorn as he could, and anytime he was around Acorn, he exaggerated his masculine manners. He intended to show Acorn by example how young men should behave. Of course, Corn Flower was almost always along, but even her manners were less effeminate than were Acorn's. Sparrow worried about Acorn. There was not much childhood left. He didn't like to think of Acorn as a grown man with the characteristics of a woman. If Acorn was going to change, it would have to be soon. But pouting there over the dead squirrel, Acorn did not show much promise.

"Even the girl's got two," said Acorn. "But not me. Oh, no. I have just one."

Corn Flower had just plucked the second dart out of the warm, soft body. She gave Sparrow a quick glance, and he thought that she read in that instant on his face all that he was thinking.

"This one is really yours, Acorn," she said. "You shot it first."

She held the squirrel by its tail out at arm's length toward Acorn. He took it without a word and tied it to his belt. Sparrow was ashamed for his friend.

"I think we should go back to Ijodi," he said. "We should take these squirrels to our mothers."

"Yes," said Acorn. "I'm tired anyway. This isn't fun anymore."

They turned and started back toward Ijodi, the town where they all lived, and they walked slowly and in silence. Acorn's poutiness had dampened the spirit of fun that had previously dominated their day. Sparrow did not really want the day to come to an end, even though he had made the suggestion. This problem with Acorn was a frustrating one. His example did not seem to be having any effect. He walked slowly and fell behind his two friends. They were all growing up. He was afraid that he would not like the way in which Acorn would mature. But Corn Flower. It suddenly struck him that Corn Flower was already beginning to look like a woman, and she was going to be a very beautiful woman. Just then she stopped and lifted a hand.

"Listen," she said.

Acorn stopped still, his eyes wide.

"What is it?" he said.

"Shh. Someone's coming."

The lane they were on wound its way through thick woods, so they could not see very far ahead. They were well within the vast domain of their own people, *Ani-yunwi-ya*, the Real People, and, in fact, they were not far from their own town of Ijodi, so there was no real reason for fear. Rather, it was a childish game they played.

"Come on," said Corn Flower in a loud whisper. "Let's hide and see who it is."

She led the way off the road and into the woods, where the three of them crouched low behind some thick brush. They waited in silence, their hearts pounding almost as if they had been deep in enemy territory. The footsteps came closer. They were heavy footsteps of a big man with a long stride. Then he came in view, and they saw the long, colorful feather cloak flapping behind him as he moved along. They saw the feather crown on his shaven head. And they knew who he was. They crouched still, their fear becoming a bit more real, the play taking on at

last a slight element of real danger. He was the single
most powerful authority among all of the towns of the
Real People. He was a figure who inspired awe and dread
among all, wherever he went. And he was seldom seen.
Soon he had walked on by. The three companions stood
up and moved uneasily back out into the road.

"That was Astugataga, wasn't it?" said Sparrow.

"Yes," said Corn Flower. "That was Standing-in-the-
Doorway, the Real Priest, the headman of *Ani-Kutani*, the
priests of Anisgayayi."

"I wonder where he's going?" said Acorn.

"He's headed back to Anisgayayi, Men's Town," said
Corn Flower. "It's back that way."

"He might be going somewhere else," said Acorn. "You
don't know for sure that he's going to Men's Town."

"All right," said Corn Flower. "Let's find out."

"How?" said Acorn.

"You mean follow him?" said Sparrow.

"Yes," said Corn Flower. "Well, not exactly. We'll cut
through the woods and get ahead of him. I know some
high rocks where we can sit and watch him. Come on."

Again she led the way. It was just habit. She made the
decisions. She led and they followed. It had been that way
for about as long as Sparrow could remember. He didn't
object. It was just the nature of their personalities that
caused the behavior. He liked her company, and he liked
the adventures into which she led them. He wasn't sure
about Acorn's reasons for following along. Perhaps Acorn
simply didn't have any other real friends. But Corn
Flower plunged into the woods, and Sparrow and Acorn
followed without question or comment. For a while all
they had to do was dodge around trees and make their
way through or around underbrush, but soon they were
climbing as well. The going got rougher and steeper. Still

Corn Flower kept up a rapid and steady pace. Sparrow was just behind her, but Acorn was falling farther behind with each stride.

They splashed across a swift-flowing mountain stream, and Acorn slipped and fell, skinning his elbow. He started to grow angry, but he scrambled to his feet and ran after his friends, the wet, dead squirrels flapping against his thigh. Then the way grew steeper yet, and they were no longer running uphill, they were climbing. At last, panting and still angry, Acorn was startled when he came right up on Corn Flower and Sparrow sitting behind a large boulder. He scowled, but he pulled himself on up beside them and sat down.

"Why are we waiting here?" he said.

"Look down there," said Corn Flower, pointing around the boulder. Acorn pulled himself up with a groan and moved to look. They were high up above the road, and from their vantage point, they could see a good long stretch of the way below. "We'll see him when he comes along here," Corn Flower concluded. Acorn sat back down.

"If we're just going to wait," he said, "you didn't have to try to run off and leave me behind."

"I didn't mean to run off and leave you," said Corn Flower. "I thought you could keep up. You're a good runner."

"Besides," said Sparrow, "I was in between. I could see you the whole time. And here we are. All three of us."

"Well," said Acorn, "where is Standing-in-the-Doorway?"

"He'll be coming along soon," said Corn Flower.

"Unless he's already gone by," said Acorn.

"We took a shortcut," said Corn Flower, "and we ran. He hasn't been by here yet."

"Maybe he's invisible," said Acorn. "A *kutani* can do that. He can do that and lots of other things. Maybe he turned into an owl, and he's flying back to Men's Town. We could wait here all night and never see him again."

"He's coming now," said Sparrow, and the other two jumped up to watch around the boulder. Standing-in-the-Doorway had not slowed his pace. He moved in long, quick strides, not looking anywhere except straight ahead. The youngsters stared in awe at the figure of dread moving along there below them.

"Let's go home," said Acorn.

"You go if you want to," said Corn Flower. "I'm going to follow him and watch him go into Men's Town."

"What if he catches us?"

"He'll cook us and eat us if he catches us," said Corn Flower, "but he won't catch us. We'll be careful."

"She's just saying that," said Sparrow. "Come on. He won't do anything to us."

They started down the mountainside toward the road again. Standing-in-the-Doorway had already passed beyond the range of vision from up by the boulder. From that, Corn Flower reasoned, he would be far enough ahead of them by the time they got back down on the road that he wouldn't know he was being followed.

"Just before he gets to Men's Town," she said, "there's another bend in the road. From there the road is straight. We can get to that bend, and then we can watch him go into the town."

"Is there some special ceremony when Standing-in-the-Doorway returns?" asked Sparrow.

"I don't know," she answered, "but we'll find out, won't we?"

They hurried down the mountainside, and although the way was steep, even Acorn managed to make it to the road without taking another tumble, but by the time he got there, Corn Flower was well ahead of him. He trotted along to catch up. At last, at a place where the road curved sharply to their right, she called a halt again. Coming up not far behind her, the boys could tell, even though they couldn't see the road beyond the curve, that up ahead was a deep valley. Down in that valley was Men's Town. They ran up to stand beside her, and just as they arrived, he appeared. They would talk about it later, and they would all agree that they had not seen him walk around the bend or out of the woods. He had simply appeared, standing there before them. His hands were on his hips, and he was looking down at them with a stern, even fierce, expression on his tattooed face. He was easily the tallest man any of them had ever seen—Standing-in-the-Doorway.

"You've been following me," he said, and his voice was deep and resonant. "Why have you been following me?"

If Corn Flower was afraid, she didn't let it show. She stepped boldly toward Standing-in-the-Doorway.

"We have a gift for you," she said. "We brought you these five squirrels."

She pulled the squirrel loose from the cord at her waist, and she turned toward her companions, holding out her hand. The boys jerked loose their squirrels, and Corn Flower took them. Turning back to face Standing-in-the-Doorway, she held out the offering. The big man looked at one young face after the other. One half of his mouth twisted into a wry smile.

"What are your names?" he said.

"I'm called Corn Flower. I'm one of *Ani-Kawi*, the Deer People, and these are my friends, Acorn and Sparrow. They're both *Ani-Tsisqua*, Bird People."

"And where do you live?"

"We live in Ijodi," she said.

Standing-in-the-Doorway reached out to take the squirrels.

"You had better go home," he said. "It will be late now by the time you get back, and your mother will be wondering about you."

Sparrow was frightened, but he had noticed something which was strange, and it was puzzling him. The *kutani* seemed only to look at Acorn, and it was a strange look, a look which Sparrow could not define. The three adventurers had not responded to the suggestion made by the high priest. They just stood seemingly mesmerized. Standing-in-the-Doorway spoke again, this time sharply.

"Go," he said.

They turned and ran. They ran as if their lives depended on their speed, and they ran until they could run no more. At last Corn Flower stopped running and stepped off the road to lean back panting against the trunk of a large oak tree. The boys stopped too. Sparrow sat on a large flat rock, and Acorn just dropped to the ground, falling over on his back. It was some time before they could catch their breath and speak again.

"Well," said Sparrow, "at least he didn't cook us and eat us."

"Corn Flower just made that up," said Acorn. "The *Ani-Kutani* don't do things like that."

"If we hadn't had squirrels to give him," said Corn Flower, "he might have taken us."

"You're just saying that," said Acorn. "You're always saying crazy things."

Sparrow glanced at Acorn. The pout was back on Acorn's face, and Sparrow thought again about the way Standing-in-the-Doorway had looked at Acorn. He wondered if Acorn had noticed that look and, if so, what he was thinking about it. Corn Flower stood up straight.

"Are you ready?" she said. "Let's go."

The boys followed her back onto the road, and they started moving again toward home, but this time they walked. Acorn kicked up puffs of dust deliberately as he walked.

"We didn't even see Men's Town," he said.

Two

IJODI HAD BEEN BUILT beside the river they called Tanasi. When they spoke to it ceremonially, they called it Yunwi-Ganahida, or Long Person, and they knew him as a man with his head resting in the mountains and his feet reaching to the lowlands, and they said that to those who could understand his language he was constantly speaking. Up above Ijodi, not far, was the creek called Sudagi. Perhaps two hundred and fifty people, Real People, lived in Ijodi in houses made of sticks and plastered with mud. The houses were rectangular in shape, perhaps four paces by five paces, perhaps a little larger. Beside each house stood an *osi*, or hot house, much smaller and dome-shaped, also plastered with mud. The side of Ijodi away from the river was lined with small family plots owned, as were the houses, by women, and one large communal garden. In these gardens grew several varieties each of corn, squash, pumpkins, gourds and beans.

The town itself was constructed around a large plaza,

and the nearest buildings to the plaza were public, the
largest of those being the townhouse. All of this, except
the gardens, was enclosed by a palisade fence which, like
the houses, was plastered with mud. There was no gate at
the entrance; rather the two ends of the fence were deliberately constructed so that they did not meet but ran parallel to each other for several yards, forming a long and
narrow passageway through which people could only pass
comfortably in single file. As the three wandering youngsters returned home, Corn Flower was the first to enter
the passageway. Sparrow followed her, and Acorn plod-
ded along in the rear. He was still sullen.

The sounds of shouting and laughter filled the town,
and they were coming from the plaza. Corn Flower
picked up the pace and led her two loyal followers to the
center of town. It seemed as if all of the men and children
and some of the women were gathered there. The
gatayusti game was in progress.

"Let's watch," said Corn Flower, and she ran to the
edge of the playing field. Da-le-danigisgi, Hemp Carrier,
Sparrow's mother's brother, was just about to make his
toss. Bets were still being made by some of the bystanders.
Hemp Carrier held in his left hand a polished stone disc,
the diameter of which just about equaled the distance
from Hemp Carrier's wrist to the tip of his middle finger.
The rims of the stone were rounded, and it was concave
on both sides. In his right hand he held an eight-foot-long
pole, sharpened on one end like a spear. Standing next to
Hemp Carrier was Yona-equa, Big Bear, the father of
Sparrow. He held a pole in his right hand similar to the
one Hemp Carrier held.

Then Hemp Carrier drew back his left arm, swung it
forward and with a mighty toss released the stone disc.
No sooner had he released it than he began to run after it,

the pole drawn back over his shoulder ready to fling. The stone hit the ground some distance ahead and began rolling like a wheel, and Hemp Carrier threw his spear. He stopped to watch its flight. The stone wheel slowed, wobbled and fell on its side, and the spear reached the end of its trajectory about the same time, stabbing itself into the soft ground just ahead of the stone. It fell back then, coming to rest on top of the disc.

A general shout went up from the crowd, and the men who had bet on Hemp Carrier began happily collecting their winnings: arrows, knives, furs. Almost anything could be used for a bet.

"No one can beat my uncle, Hemp Carrier," said Sparrow. "He's the best in Ijodi at *gatayusti.*"

"You're always bragging," said Acorn.

Sparrow felt the skin on his face grow hot. He really didn't think it was bragging to express pride in the accomplishments of someone else, and even though his uncle was a winner, it was his father who had lost. Still, he decided not to respond to Acorn's remark. Acorn was pouty and sullen enough already.

"Do you know anyone who can beat Hemp Carrier?" asked Corn Flower.

Acorn pretended not to hear.

"I have to go home," he said, and he turned and walked away without another word.

"What's the matter with Acorn today?" said Corn Flower.

"I don't know," said Sparrow. "I'm worried about him, though. He's my friend, but I don't like the way he's been acting lately. I don't know what to do about it, though."

"There's nothing you can do about it."

"I just try to act right and hope that he notices."

"He's too old, Sparrow," said Corn Flower. "He's already formed his ways. He won't change now."

Sparrow hoped that Corn Flower was wrong, but he didn't say anything more. She was probably right, he thought. He hated to admit it, even to himself, but she was probably right.

Wild Hemp was cooking in front of the house when Sparrow arrived back home. The boy sat down on a short tree stump beside the door to watch her.

"You were out a long time today," said his mother.

"Yes," he answered.

"Were you with your friends?"

"Yes. Acorn and Corn Flower were with me. We hunted for squirrels."

Wild Hemp looked at her son and then looked around as if she were searching for something that should have been there.

"I don't see any," she said. "You didn't bring me any squirrels after such a long day of hunting?"

"No," said Sparrow. "I got some, but I gave them away."

Just then Big Bear walked up.

"I have just lost everything to my brother-in-law," he said. "Now I'm a poor man. I'll have to start all over and make new things."

"That happens to you every time you play against my brother," said Wild Hemp. "You never learn."

"Oh, I don't mind. Besides, he's a challenge for me. I keep thinking that one day I just might beat him."

"Ha," said Wild Hemp.

"Did I hear you asking about squirrels?" said Big Bear, and he looked toward his son. "Did you hunt all day and bring back nothing?"

"I killed two squirrels," said Sparrow. "Corn Flower also killed two, and Acorn killed one, but Acorn was grumbling so, Corn Flower gave him one of hers. I'm ashamed of him, the way he's been acting."

"I've seen him lately," said Big Bear. "He's going to grow up to be a man-woman, I think."

"I've been trying to show him how a man is supposed to behave," said Sparrow, "but it doesn't seem to be doing any good."

"He's nearly grown," said Big Bear. "You can't do anything about it now. Besides, if that's the way he's supposed to be, no one could do anything anyway."

"So where are your squirrels?" said Wild Hemp.

Sparrow sat silent for a moment. Then he told them about the meeting with Standing-in-the-Doorway. He told about the game they played and how they got caught and finally about the clever way in which Corn Flower got them out of trouble by giving away their squirrels.

"I wonder what that *kutani* was doing away from Men's Town," said Big Bear.

"The food is ready," said Wild Hemp. "Let's eat."

She dished out the meal for the three of them, and the conversation came to a halt while they ate venison and beans and squash. When they had finished, they sat back to relax. The sun was already dropping behind the mountains.

"Before the *gatayusti* game," said Big Bear, "I was over visiting with my clansmen, the Blue People, *Ani-Sakonige*. We were talking about the *Ani-Kutani*. Some of the older men said the priests seem to have much more power now than before. Some of them were wondering if it's right."

"There's going to be a big ball play in a few days," said Wild Hemp, adroitly changing the direction of the talk.

"Maybe Standing-in-the-Doorway was just out selecting the field."

"That's right," said Big Bear. "That would be his function."

"Who's going to play?" said Sparrow.

"Some *Ani-Chahta* are coming," said Wild Hemp.

"There's a dispute over some land between our towns and theirs," said Big Bear. "*Aneja*, the little brother of war, the ball play, will decide the outcome."

"The winners will own the land?" said Sparrow.

"Yes," said Big Bear. "If the Choctaws win, it will be their land. If the Real People win, it will be ours. It's good hunting land. It's an important fight, so your mother is probably right. Standing-in-the-Doorway was probably selecting the field."

"Or doctoring it," said Wild Hemp, "to make sure we win."

"Where will they play?" said Sparrow.

"Near Kituwah, I think," said Big Bear. "They won't announce the exact site until just before the game. That way the Choctaws won't get a chance to doctor it for themselves. We'll just go to Kituwah on the right morning and wait until they announce the place for the game. Then we'll go out there with everyone else to watch."

Kituwah, one of the old mother towns of the Real People, was crowded that day, and even more people were gathered outside of the town. The Choctaws were there too. The town itself was constructed much like Ijodi, and, like Ijodi, was surrounded by a palisade fence. Well beyond the fence several ball fields were laid out where *aneja* could be played. Really there was not much to be laid out. The game would be played on an open field with no boundaries on the sides. A goal would be indicated at each end of the field just before the start of the game, and no one would know exactly where the field would be until the goals were set. This was a precaution against the common practice of conjurers making medicine on the field, before the game, against the opposition.

Sparrow had gone to Kituwah with his family, but soon he had found his friends Corn Flower and Acorn, and the three wandered about on their own, looking at the crowds of people and joining in the general spirit of excitement and enthusiasm.

"Look," said Acorn, pointing. "Are those the Choctaws?"

"I think so," said Sparrow.

"Have you ever seen a Choctaw before?"

"No."

"I have," said Corn Flower. "Those are Choctaws."

"Look over there," Acorn shouted, gesturing toward a large group of nearly naked men returning to the fields from the direction of the river.

"It's the ball players," said Corn Flower. "They've gone to the water, and they've been scratched."

The three companions ran toward the ball players. Then they stopped and watched as the players walked past them. They could see the blood-red streaks down the backs of the men, the fresh scratches made by the doctors to make them run faster, and on some of the men, they could see the bodies of bats dangling from their belts. Each man carried two ballsticks, one in each hand, sticks about as long as their arms bent on one end and laced with rawhide to form them into rackets. At the edge of the vast clearing from which a playing field would be selected, the players stopped and stood waiting in a cluster. There were twenty-five or thirty of them. Then from the crowd of Choctaws a group of players emerged.

From somewhere in the back of the crowd of Real People, near the entrance to the town of Kituwah, a general shout arose. Everyone looked in that direction, and the crowd could be seen parting to clear a path. In a short while, Sparrow saw the reason. Four men were walking through the crowd carrying on their shoulders the long poles that supported the chair in which Standing-in-the-Doorway sat. One man walked before the litter, two others walked, one on each side, carrying three long willow branches each. Another man walked behind. The people grew silent and watched as Standing-in-the-Doorway was borne far into the clearing. The bearers stopped for a moment. Standing-in-the-Doorway said something in a low voice, and they turned to their left and carried him farther. He stopped them again and pointed to a spot on the ground to his right. One of the men with the willow branches moved quickly to that spot and jammed one end of a long branch into the ground. He stepped off four wide paces and stuck a second branch into the ground. That left him with one long willow switch. That would be the mark of his official capacity during the game. He would be one of two drivers.

Standing-in-the-Doorway spoke again, and his bearers carried him one hundred and twenty paces away from the goal. There the other driver set up the other goal. The playing field was defined. For a team to score, they must get the ball between the two willow branches at the opposite end of the field from which they began play. The two other men, the one who had led the way and the one who had followed, took up positions behind the goals. These were the scorekeepers. As Standing-in-the-Doorway was carried off to one side of the field, the two drivers met in the center for a quick conference. Then one of them ran toward a goal.

"Real People," he called, and the players of the Real People shouted and ran after him, taking their positions on the field. The other driver ran toward the opposite goal.

"Choctaw People," he shouted as he ran. The Choctaw players followed him. With the teams in place, the two drivers met again in the center of the field and ran together to stand before Standing-in-the-Doorway, still in his chair, at the side of the field. Sparrow and his two friends had found themselves a spot at the front of the crowd nearby. They watched as Standing-in-the-Doorway produced the ball from beneath his great feathered cloak. It was a hard ball sewn of deerhide, small enough for a man of average size to almost hide inside a closed fist. Standing-in-the-Doorway held the ball for a moment before his eyes. He looked from one driver to the other. Then he tossed the ball to the shortest of the two.

"Start the game," he said.

The drivers ran out into the field again, and they called the two teams together. The driver with the ball stood in the center. The other moved to one side and took a deep breath.

"Let the game begin," he shouted, and the driver in the center tossed the ball straight up into the air as high as he could, and he ran for his life as the two teams rushed toward each other swinging their sticks and clamoring for the elusive ball.

Three

THEY FOUGHT FURIOUSLY for most of the day. About midday some of the spectators left to eat. Others endured the hunger and kept watching the game. One of the Real People suffered a broken nose when a Choctaw swung his stick and hit him across the face. He had continued playing, though, until the swelling and the pain had almost blinded him. Then he went out and sat dejected alongside the field. The Real People soon balanced the numbers again by breaking the arm of a Choctaw, thus sending him out of the game. Almost all of the players on the field were bloody.

And the scoring was high. Once a Choctaw grabbed the ball up and saw before him a long stretch of open field. He dropped his sticks, put the ball in his mouth and ran for the goal. Everyone was after him, but no one touched him, and he scored, and his score tied the game. The players were all good. In spite of himself, Sparrow admired even the Choctaw players.

He did wonder, though, why the Choctaws had included one man on their team. He was fat and clumsy and slow, and he didn't really seem to be even trying to accomplish anything. He just stood off to one side and watched. Like all of the other players, he held a ballstick in each hand, but he just stood there letting his sticks dangle at his sides, watching.

But there was a man playing for the Real People who was, Sparrow thought, a real ball player. Sparrow had never seen anyone run so fast as this man. And he was quick, too, darting this way and that. He scored the first four points for the Real People. Then Sparrow discovered the fat Choctaw's purpose. The fast runner for the Real People had the ball once more. He had dropped his sticks, and he was running, the ball clutched firmly in his left hand. A group of Choctaws moved to head him off, and he dodged to his left, moving just close enough to the fat Choctaw, who swung out one heavy arm at just the right moment to catch the runner around his chest. The runner threw the ball just as the fat Choctaw enfolded him tight in both of his own arms. And they stood there like that, the Choctaw with his arms reaching around from behind holding out of the game the fastest runner on the team of the Real People.

Still the team of the Real People was the best Sparrow had ever seen. He did not know any of the players. There was no one from Ijodi on the team. It was being said throughout the crowd that the team had been handpicked by Standing-in-the-Doorway from towns throughout the wide domain of the Real People, and most of the players had come from remote towns like Nikutsegi, Dagunahi and Dahlonega. One of the players was from Kituwah, and one was actually a priest from Men's Town. He was a short, squat man with a funny, round face, and Sparrow at last overheard the man's name: Iya-Iyusdi, Like-a-Pumpkin.

It was late afternoon, and one more score would win the game for the Real People. The ball was loose deep in the territory of the Real People, and players from both sides ran after it. A Choctaw tried to scoop it up with his sticks, but he was hit from behind by a Real Person, and he fell on the ball. The man who had knocked him down fell on top of him, and as they struggled for control of the ball, others threw themselves down and joined in the tussle. Soon there was a pile of players on top of the ball. Those players not in the pile circled menacingly. The game was going nowhere. It was effectively stopped until the two drivers with their willow switches rushed in and began lashing at the pile of nearly naked bodies tangled together, and as a player felt the lash, he would yelp, extricate himself and run off to the side.

Soon the pile was no more, and the Choctaw with the ball stood up. He looked desperately around and found himself surrounded by the enemy, so he made a high toss for the goal. One of the Real People knocked the ball out of the air with his stick, and another grabbed it up and began to run for the opposite goal. Choctaws appeared before him, and he was about to be overwhelmed when he saw, far ahead and all alone close to the goal, the little priest, Like-a-Pumpkin. He made a mighty toss over the heads of all the players. They turned to follow the ball, and they watched in astonishment as the funny-looking man reached up with his long ballsticks and plucked the flying missile out of the air with seeming ease, then turned and ran the few steps to carry the ball between the upright willow branches.

The game was over, and the Real People had won. The Choctaw players flung themselves to the ground and moaned and wailed their loss, while the Real People, players and spectators alike, set up a howl of joy and satisfaction and pride and triumph. Sparrow dared a glance toward Standing-in-the-Doorway, and he thought that he could see just a hint of satisfaction in the expression of the *kutani*, but it lasted only an instant. And then Sparrow saw the eyes of Standing-in-the-Doorway shift toward Acorn, and he saw again the look that had troubled him so before. He felt a chill run up his spine, and he looked quickly back to the ball field, and he began to shout with the rest of the crowd.

It was the morning of the following day, and the Choctaws, dejected, were returning home. Three ball players were particularly morose. One was the last Choctaw to have had the ball, and some were saying that he should have scored. Some had gone so far as to say that he had lost the game for the Choctaws. His name was Panther, and his companions in misery were called Fox Skin and Crawling Snake. All three had played well, and they all suffered equally the normal dejection that comes with a hard-fought loss. But in addition to that, they were made angry by the jeers of some of their traveling companions. Slowly they dropped back until they were at last alone on the road. Then they stopped and sat together to seethe and sulk and allow their tormentors to get well ahead of them.

"They'll start all over again when we reach home," said Fox Skin.

"At least we won't have to endure their taunts along the way," said Crawling Snake.

"I don't want to have to endure them along the way or back home," said Panther, "and I don't mean to endure them."

The other two looked at him for a brief moment, puzzled. What could he mean? They could see no way to avoid the taunting, only to delay it by traveling home alone.

"Are you planning something, Panther?" said Fox Skin.

"Yes. I'm not going home. Not just yet. I'm going back almost where we just came from, but I'm not going to the *Chalakee* town of Kituwah. Just before I get there, I'll leave the road and go around the town. The road runs on until it comes to another *Chalakee* town, one they call Ijodi. I'll watch that road. There should be lots of traveling back and forth, and if I watch long enough, someone will come along."

"Then what?" said Crawling Snake.

"Who knows? It depends on who comes along. If it's a warrior, I'll kill him and take home a scalp. If it's women or children, I may take them captive. One way or another, I will go home with a warrior's trophy. That will stop the taunts."

"I'll go with you," said Crawling Snake.

"And I," said Fox Skin.

Sparrow, Acorn and Corn Flower were away from Ijodi again. They were not hunting, not doing anything in particular. They carried their blowguns, but they just walked casually along the road, the one that, if they walked it long enough, would take them back to Kituwah and eventually on into Choctaw country. They had been talking about the excitement of the previous day, recalling spectacular plays in the game and naming their favorite players. At last they all agreed that their favorite was the funny little priest who had won the day for the Real People with his amazing catch.

"What was his name?" said Acorn.

"Pumpkin," said Sparrow. "Like-a-Pumpkin."

"Yes," said Corn Flower. "That was it."

"But they were all good," said Sparrow. "Even the Choctaws had good players."

"The Choctaws were no good," said Acorn. "Our people beat them, didn't they?"

"Of course they did," said Corn Flower, "but it was a close game. If the Choctaws were no good, the game would have been over with quickly."

Acorn couldn't think of a worthwhile response to Corn Flower's assertion, so he looked at the ground, walked a little more slowly and shoved his lower lip out just a bit. Then he almost ran into her back when she stopped abruptly, holding up a hand to indicate a halt. She gestured with her chin to point out something in the path ahead. The two boys looked to see what it was she had spotted, and there in the middle of their way just about ten paces ahead was coiled *ujonati*, the rattlesnake. Acorn grabbed up a rock and threw it. It came close, but it missed, and *ujonati* slithered to the side of the road and vanished into the deep leaves of the forest floor.

"Acorn," said Corn Flower, speaking sharply, "why did you do that? You know better than that."

"*Ujonati* is good," said Sparrow. "He won't bite us so long as we leave him alone. We pray to him."

"And you know what will happen if you harm him, or worse, if you kill him," said Corn Flower. "His relatives will seek revenge on us. You know the story about the rattlesnake's revenge. Everyone knows it."

"A man went out hunting," said Sparrow, "and while he was gone, his wife, back home, went outside for something or other. A rattlesnake was there, and it surprised her. Before she had time to think, she killed it with a stick."

"Just then," said Corn Flower, taking over the story, "the hunter out in the woods found himself suddenly surrounded by rattlesnakes, a whole clan. The leader, their chief, stood up real tall, and he spoke to the man. He said, 'Your wife has just now killed my brother. Go home and send her outside for water. I'll be waiting out there to get my revenge. If you refuse to do this, we'll just kill you right now.' So the man agreed."

"And he did it," said Sparrow. "He did what the rattlesnake told him to do, and the rattlesnake killed the woman."

Acorn was looking at the ground again.

"I know the story," he said. "I don't know why I threw the rock. Anyway, I didn't hit him, did I?"

Sparrow started to feel sorry for Acorn. Maybe he had been chastised enough, and Sparrow didn't want him to become angry and pout for the rest of the day.

"I guess you're right," he said. "No harm was done after all. We three are always getting into something we shouldn't anyway, aren't we? We're like *ani-chuja*, the boys."

"You mean the Little Thunders?" said Acorn, a grin spreading across his face.

"Yes," said Sparrow.

"We're not like the boys," said Corn Flower. "There were two of them, and there are three of us."

"But when their brother Lightning came, then there were three," said Acorn.

"Yes," said Corn Flower, "but they were three boys. I'm a girl. And besides that, the boys killed their mother. I could never do that."

"I could," said Acorn. "If my mother was a witch. Their mother was a witch."

"They *thought* she was a witch," said Corn Flower.

"She was Selu, Corn, the mother of all corn, and she feeds us still."

Sparrow looked at Acorn and saw a hard coldness in his face that he had never seen there before. He thought of the look on the face of Standing-in-the-Doorway when he had looked at Acorn, and he wondered if something could have been transferred from the priest to his friend by that terrible look. He shuddered at the idea. He shook the unpleasantness out of his mind with the thought that, after all, Corn Flower was right about the story. She was certainly not like a boy. Far from it. She was a girl who was on the verge of becoming a woman, and she would be a beautiful woman. He looked at her, a quick glance, and he was embarrassed at his thoughts. No, not thoughts. Feelings. They were too vague to be called thoughts. He did not quite understand these uncomfortable feelings that suddenly and unexpectedly stirred within him, feelings regarding his lifelong playmate Corn Flower, and he wished that they would go away. There was something somehow ominous about those feelings.

"I guess you're right," he said to her.

"About what?"

"About the boys. I guess we're more like the boy and his family and friends in the story of the bears."

"The story about where the bears came from?" she said.

"Yes. That one."

"Why?" said Acorn.

"I know," said Corn Flower. "Because we stay out so long. Just like the boy in that story. He stayed out in the woods playing all day. Each day he stayed longer, and his mother worried. She asked him not to stay out so long, but he said that he liked it out there. She worried that he missed his meals, but he said that he could find plenty to eat in the woods. Finally one day he came home long after dark, and his mother said, 'I don't want you to stay gone so long anymore.' But the boy said, 'Tomorrow when I go out, I think that I won't come back at all. I'll just stay there to live.'

" 'But we'll miss you,' said his mother.

" 'Then come with me,' said the boy. 'There's plenty to eat for all of us.' "

"So the next day," said Sparrow, "the boy and his mother and father and all of his family went to the woods. Some of their neighbors saw them going and asked them what they were doing. They told them and said that there was plenty of food out there. 'You can come with us,' they said, and some of them did, but the others stayed in their town and watched them go."

"And just before they disappeared into the woods," said Corn Flower, "the people saw them changing, and they had become the bears."

"I'm not like that," said Acorn. "I don't want to live in the woods and eat nothing but acorns and hickory nuts and berries. And right now, I want to go home. I'm tired of all this."

Acorn turned and started walking back toward Ijodi.

"Acorn," said Sparrow, "it's early yet. Don't go."

"Let him go," said Corn Flower. "He'll just be pouting the rest of the day anyway."

They stood for a moment watching Acorn as he walked away. He disappeared around a curve in the road.

"Come on," said Corn Flower. "Let's go down to the river."

Sparrow suddenly felt ill at ease. He didn't like it that Acorn was leaving them in his sullen mood, but even more, he realized, he did not want to be left alone with Corn Flower, not since the strange new feelings had descended upon him. Not just yet anyway. He wasn't at all sure that he was ready to be anything more to Corn Flower than he had always been, her friend, companion and playmate. And then, he had no idea what she would think when she heard about these new feelings.

"No," he said. "Acorn's spoiled the day for me now. Let's just follow him back to Ijodi."

When they came around the bend in the road, they saw him, his eyes wide with terror. He was standing in the middle of the road facing them, a big Choctaw just behind him holding him tight by his long scalplock and touching a knife to his throat. The Choctaw was smiling. Sparrow recognized the man from the ball play. He was the last Choctaw to have touched the ball. Sparrow and Corn Flower glanced quickly at one another. They were standing still in the road wondering what to do, when, one from each side and slightly to their rear, two more Choctaws stepped into the road.

Four

W E HAVE TO GO BACK the way we came," Panther said to his comrades. "We don't want to be seen by any *Chalakees* from Kituwah."

Sparrow listened carefully, but he did not understand the Choctaw language. He did, however, recognize the word *"Chalakee,"* the word the Choctaws used to designate the Real People, and he recognized the name "Kituwah" even the way the Choctaw pronounced it. He knew the Choctaws had to get past Kituwah in order to get back to their own country, so he figured that was what the man had been talking about. Then, sure enough, the Choctaws, having tied the hands of their three captives behind their backs, pushed them off the road in order to work their way around the town through the woods. Walking through the woods, one of the Choctaws gave Sparrow a shove and spoke to him roughly.

"I don't understand," said Sparrow, and the Choctaw responded again in his own language. So, Sparrow thought, they don't speak my language, and none of us can speak theirs. He knew that the Choctaws could probably speak the Mobilian trade language. It was, after all, based on their own tongue. Many of the Real People could use it too, but Sparrow knew only a few words, and he decided not to let on that he knew any of it.

By mid-afternoon they had worked their way around Kituwah and were headed back for the road. Sparrow had tried a few times to talk to Corn Flower or to Acorn, but each time he received rough blows from one or more of his captors. They were walking along a ridge that would take them back to the road. It was a longer way along the ridge, but the way down the side was steep and treacherous. The Choctaws had been hurrying, pushing their captives along, but comfortably past Kituwah, they relaxed a little and slowed the pace. At last they stopped for a rest, and the three captives sat down on the ground. The Choctaws laid aside the three blowguns they had taken from Sparrow and his friends. They were armed still with their own knives and warclubs.

"Sparrow," said Acorn, his voice trembling, "what are we going to do?"

One of the Choctaws spoke sharply and kicked Acorn across the back with the side of his foot. Sparrow made a quick decision. He might be able to trick the Choctaws into believing that someone was nearby to help the captives.

"Uncle," he shouted. "Hemp Carrier. We're over here. Choctaws have got us. Three of them."

The Choctaws all turned to Sparrow. They saw that he was looking back toward Kituwah, and they all shot quick, nervous glances in that direction. They had not understood his words, but they had gotten the idea that Sparrow was calling for help. Panther turned back on Sparrow angrily as Sparrow scrambled to his feet, his back to the steep drop. Panther pulled his heavy wooden warclub from his belt and took a wild swing at Sparrow. Sparrow dodged to his right, and the warclub burned his left shoulder. His movement carried him back, and he fell, sliding and tumbling out of control down the steep side of the mountain. The Choctaws watched him for a moment, talked among themselves hurriedly, then seemed to shrug him off as lost but unimportant. They pulled Corn Flower and Acorn to their feet and pushed them on their way along the ridge. They did not bother to pick up the blowguns.

Sparrow lay still, afraid to move. He didn't know if the Choctaws were pursuing him or not. At least, he figured, not all three would come after him. One or two would have to remain behind to watch the other two captives. His breathing was fast and heavy, and he thought that it was loud. He wondered if the Choctaws could hear him. He ached all over from cuts, scratches and bruises resulting from his long tumble over the rocks and through bramble and brush. After what seemed to him a long wait, he decided to risk movement. He rolled over so he could get up on his knees. Nothing seemed to be broken, and for that he was thankful. He raised himself up slowly and looked toward the ridge from which he had toppled. He saw no one. He stood up. Still he saw no one. They must have gone on without him. His hands were still tied behind him, but he was free. He was free, but his two friends were not.

Sparrow stood for a moment wondering what to do. He could run back to Kituwah for help, but how much farther ahead might the Choctaws get in the time that would take? Could he afford the time? He decided that he could not, and he began to work on the thongs that bound his wrists. He twisted his hands in an attempt to loosen them, but the thongs simply bit into his wrists. He looked around desperately then until he spotted a large rock partially embedded in the ground. It had sharp edges, and he sat down, backing up to the rock. It took a while, but he finally managed to cut himself free. Then he climbed back up the steep hillside. There he saw the three blowguns abandoned on the ridge. He gathered the darts from the guns of his two friends and added them to those already tucked into a small pouch which dangled from his own blowgun. Taking the blowgun and all the darts, he started in pursuit of the Choctaws and his friends.

He moved with an easy trot. He wanted to catch them, but he didn't want to run up on them unexpectedly and unprepared. As he moved, his mind wandered. He tried to focus his thoughts. He needed to figure out what to do when he did catch up to them. He was still a boy, and he was in pursuit of three full-grown men, ball players and warriors. The men were armed with knives and warclubs, and Sparrow carried a blowgun and darts, a child's weapon. A weapon to hunt small birds. He would have to plan. He would have to use stealth.

But he couldn't think clearly as he ran. He recalled his new, troubling feelings for Corn Flower, and it came to him that these three men, her captors, could easily have feelings too. She was nearly grown, almost a woman. Some people might even think that she was already ripe for marriage. He hoped that the Choctaws were still in enough of a hurry to get safely out of the territory of the Real People that they had not yet had time for such thoughts.

And he wondered what Corn Flower would do. She was not one to submit quietly to captivity or anything else. She was almost certain to attempt to escape, or, if the

Choctaws tried to do anything to her, to fight. He was afraid that she would get hurt if he didn't catch them soon enough. He wasn't worried that Acorn would try anything. Acorn would just do as the Choctaws told him to do. His only form of resistance would be to pout and sulk.

The ridge along which Sparrow ran was for a distance parallel with the road below, but gradually it widened, flattened and sloped downward while the road continued winding its way uphill. Sparrow could see up ahead where the two converged. He slowed his pace as he approached the road. He stopped. He could see no one. He walked out into the road, and there he found footprints which he took to be those of the three Choctaws and their captives. If he was right, they were ahead of him on the road, and they were indeed on their way to the Choctaw country.

He started after them again, again at a trot, but each time he approached a curve in the road which obscured his line of vision straight ahead, he slowed to a walk and rounded the curve with caution. He continued to see what he believed to be the tracks of the Choctaws and of Corn Flower and Acorn. He did not know how far ahead of him they might be.

The sun was more than halfway across her path on the underside of the sky vault, and Sparrow was feeling annoying pangs of hunger from deep down in his stomach. He could see berry bushes alongside the road, and he knew that the forest floor was matted thick with nuts. He thought of the boy in the story of the bears, and he ran on. His stomach would have to wait. His business was more urgent than was his hunger.

Corn Flower was determined to do something about her situation. She didn't yet know what she would do, what she could do, but she was determined not to be taken into a Choctaw town a docile, submissive captive. She was equally determined that no Choctaw man would have his way with her. There were three men she would have to deal with somehow, each one armed, each one strong, and she had no help. Not really. She could not count on Acorn, she knew. And she had no idea what had become of Sparrow after his fall. He had gone down an awfully steep mountainside with his hands tied behind his back. The mountainside, too, was cluttered with rocks, scattered trees and tangled brush. If the fall had not killed him, it had likely broken some bones. She hoped that Sparrow was not lying somewhere on that hillside hurt, twisted, alone and helpless.

She watched her captors as they moved along, studying their movements and their habits, their personalities. She knew which one was the leader, which was the most nervous, which had the quickest temper. Sometime, someplace, she would get her chance, she thought. They could not stay constantly alert. Her biggest problem, she thought, would be Acorn. If he did not help her when the time came, she would have to save him as well as herself. And she did not expect him to be any help. No. He would more likely prove to be a hindrance. Yet she knew that she would not be able to abandon him.

"I'm tired, and I'm hungry," wailed Acorn. "My feet hurt."

One of the Choctaws snapped out an order of some kind and struck Acorn across the back. Acorn whined but trudged on in silence.

Corn Flower looked at the sun in the sky. It was late afternoon. She figured the Choctaws would keep moving until dark or nearly so. They probably meant to get as far away from the towns of the Real People as possible before they stopped to rest.

. . . .

Sparrow first saw the smoke from their fire. He took to the woods and worked his way close to their camp behind the cover of trees and brush. It would be dark soon. Already it was dark underneath the thick branches of the tall trees. As close as he dared to get, Sparrow settled down for a time to observe. Corn Flower and Acorn seemed to be all right. The Choctaws were preparing a meal. From where he crouched, Sparrow couldn't tell what it was, but he guessed that they were cooking either a squirrel or a rabbit, and they seemed to be eating berries and nuts as well. They untied the captives and let them eat.

Sparrow considered looking for something to eat for himself, but he decided to wait and watch a little longer. Soon the Choctaws retied their captives, put out their fire with dirt and resumed their journey. Sparrow had hoped that they were camped for the night, but apparently such was not the case. They were going on in spite of the darkness. It would be more difficult to follow them, to stay close enough not to lose them, yet far enough back not to be detected by the Choctaws.

They moved on, and Sparrow followed. He was glad for one reason that they had elected to travel at night. As long as they were moving along, they wouldn't be trying anything with Corn Flower.

It wasn't long before Sparrow realized that the Choctaws intended to travel all night. He lost all sense of time, and it took all of his determination to keep himself going. He thought more than once how easy it would be to lie down and rest for a while. Just for a short while. Then he could get up refreshed and easily catch up with them again. But he forced himself to keep going. More than once he woke up with a start to realize that he had been walking in his sleep, and one time he almost walked up on the Choctaws. He stopped still, his heart pounding, and he waited for them to get a little farther ahead again. He shook his head violently, trying to drive out the sleepiness. He had to be more careful, had to stay awake.

At long last he saw some light in the eastern sky along the horizon. The sun had completed her journey across the top of the sky vault and had reemerged in the east on the underside. He dropped back some, slowing his pace again as the day dawned. Then, rounding a curve in the road, he saw that they had stopped again. They seemed to be preparing a camp just beside the road. Again he took to the woods, circling around to find a spot from which he could safely observe the camp. He was ahead of them and across the road. He watched. He saw them check the bonds on the wrists of Corn Flower and Acorn. He saw two of the Choctaws stretch out on the ground. After traveling most of a day and all of one night, they felt safe. They were going to rest. Now Sparrow, too, could rest.

Five

SPARROW FOUND HIMSELF a spot on the ground which looked like it could be made reasonably comfortable and stretched himself out. He knew that he could not afford to sleep too long, to let the Choctaws wake up before he did, but he needed to sleep. He couldn't take them on the way he was. His whole body ached. He thought about how he might sneak into the camp to rescue his friends. He would need a knife to cut them free and to protect himself if the Choctaws should wake up. Perhaps he could steal a knife from one of the sleeping enemy. It would be a risky thing to try, he thought. And he was tired. So tired. He felt a little guilty, lying there, allowing his eyes to close, knowing that his friends were just over there across the road, captive and bound. But as sleep overcame his body, the sense of guilt fled, chased away by fearful images of violence and danger.

He found himself naked and unarmed in the midst of the ball game. The ball lay on the ground between his feet, but he couldn't move his arms, couldn't make his hands reach for the ball. And he had no ballsticks. He should have had ballsticks. That worried him. Then three Choctaws, armed with knives and clubs, rushed at the ball and at him from the other end of the field. It was as if there were two games going on. A large game raged all around, yet he seemed to be alone against the three players who were closing in on him. No one else on the field seemed to be at all interested in what was happening there. The Choctaws were tattooed and painted and bedecked with the feathers of pheasants and ravens and owls, and their mouths were opened wide, and they were shrieking out fearful war cries. Just as they were about to smash into him, he ducked, and then he was falling, hurtling through black, empty space. He thought that he must have fallen through a hole in the earth, and he knew that there would be nothing beneath him but the chaotic underworld, the world with its days and nights and its seasons just the opposite of the world in which he lived, the world which was populated with frightful creatures, creatures that had once walked the middle earth but had in time long past moved down below, creatures like the giant hawk, *tlanuwa*, and like the powerful and terrible *uk'ten'*, the giant snake with antlers and wings, whose mere look could kill. He opened his mouth to call for help, but no sound came out.

Then he was suddenly awake, sitting up on the hard ground there close to the road and in the woods, listening to the sounds of chattering squirrels and twittering birds in the branches above his head. In a moment he remembered where he was and why he was there. He heard no sounds from the camp. He peered cautiously through the brush, and he could see that all five people over there were still stretched out on the ground. The sun was still low in the eastern sky. He lay back down, and soon he was asleep again.

The Choctaws were on their feet, naked and visibly lustful. They snarled and drooled like wild animals as they moved toward Corn Flower, tied and helpless on the ground. A few feet away, Acorn sat, seemingly disinterested. Sparrow shouted at the Choctaws, telling them to leave her alone, threatening to kill them, but no one seemed to hear him or even know that he was there. Then Standing-in-the-Doorway appeared from out of nowhere to stare at him with a look of disdain.

Back in Ijodi, Wild Hemp had gone to see Ayasta, the Spoiler, the mother of Corn Flower. Sparrow had been gone from home since sometime the morning before. He had stayed out long days before, but always he had come home before dark. This time he had not come back before dark, and the night was over. It was morning again, and there was still no sign of her son. Usually he was with Corn Flower and Acorn, so Wild Hemp had gone to see the Spoiler.

"My daughter has not returned either," the Spoiler said. She was a big-boned woman who looked as if she could hold her own in a fight with any man, and she had, in fact, won war honors in her youth in a battle with some Shawnee people, yet she was not unattractive. She was a widow who had not yet chosen to remarry. Some people talked about her behind her back. They said that the men were probably all afraid of her. Her face on this particular morning wore a troubled expression. "Have you spoken to the mother of Acorn?" she asked.

"I have come straight to you," said Wild Hemp.

"Well then," said the Spoiler, "let's go see her."

When they discovered that Acorn, too, was missing, the two women knew that something was wrong.

"Let's send our men to look for them right away," said the Spoiler.

"Yes," said Wild Hemp. "We'll meet back at the townhouse."

In a short while they had gathered: Wild Hemp, her husband Big Bear, and her brother Hemp Carrier, along with the Spoiler and her brother Agili, He-Is-Rising, and her son, Corn Flower's older brother, Dasuntali, Stinging Ant.

"Something has happened to them," said the Spoiler. "Otherwise they would have come home."

"What could have happened?" said Big Bear. "An accident might have happened to one, but not to all three."

"Perhaps," said Stinging Ant, "they've just decided that they're all grown up now, and they stayed away all this time just to tell us so."

"No," said Wild Hemp. "They wouldn't do that. At least Sparrow would not. I know."

"Nor would Corn Flower," said the Spoiler, giving her son a hard look. He ducked his head and stared at the ground.

"The Choctaw ball players were not happy when they left Kituwah," said Hemp Carrier.

There was a pause in the conversation. No one wanted to be the first to further articulate the implications of Hemp Carrier's statement. The Spoiler looked at her brother Agili.

"I think that you should go after them," she said, "and go prepared for battle, just in case."

"I'll go," Agili said.

"And I will go with you," said Stinging Ant.

"I and my brother-in-law will go," said Hemp Carrier,

with a gesture of the chin toward Big Bear, who nodded his assent. "We'll find them, and we'll bring them back."

Sparrow was awake before the Choctaws. They had eaten, he told himself, and it was the gnawing hunger pains that had awakened him. He moved carefully, going deeper into the woods to look for food. It didn't take him long. Berries and nuts were abundant. A squirrel scolded him from up above, and he looked at it.

"I can't take the time to kill you and cook you, *saloli*," he said. "Because of the Choctaws, you'll live a little longer."

Saloli chattered back, but Sparrow didn't understand. He continued gathering berries and stuffing them into his mouth. It was not a satisfying meal, but it took the sharp edge off his hunger, and soon he crept back to his post beside the road. He tried to determine how far along her path the sun had traveled, but from where he squatted at the edge of the woods, he could not be sure. He guessed that about half of the morning was gone. The Choctaws were still sleeping.

Hemp Carrier, Stinging Ant, Big Bear, Agili and two other men, Kick Up, from the Deer People, and Mocking Crows, from the Bird People, were gathered together, each well armed. The Spoiler had brought Gone-in-the-Water, a conjurer, to meet with them.

"These men are going to look for our children," she said, "but we are afraid that they may have been taken by some Choctaws."

She did not bother to say the rest of what was bothering her. The conjurer would know. If these men were only a search party looking for lost children, they might need his advice as a finder of lost things. He would consult his *uluhnsadi*, the rare and valuable transparent crystal taken from the forehead of the *ukitena*, the great anomalous creature from the chaotic underworld, and the crystal would show him the way. Then he would tell them where to look. He would do that for them. He had looked at his crystal already and talked to it before meeting with them. But there was more that was needed, and he knew it.

If the children had indeed been taken by Choctaws, then these men would be going out as warriors, to fight, perhaps to kill. For that, special ceremonial preparations were called for, and they took time. The children had been gone a day and a night and half a morning. The search party, or rescue party, would not have time for a full ceremony.

Gone-in-the-Water had weighed all this in his mind before showing himself. He knew what he was going to do. He had decided that in an emergency such as this, he could greatly abbreviate the rites of preparation for war. Of course, the warriors would all have to undergo the standard purification ceremony upon their return. He would get ready for that during their absence.

He filled his long clay pipe with a special tobacco mixture and lit it with a hot coal which he had carried in a clay pot. As he smoked, he walked around each of the six men. Now and then he stopped and said some words, speaking so quietly that not even those standing closest to him could understand them clearly.

Almost everyone who lived in Ijodi had come out to watch. The word had spread rapidly through the town, and they all knew what was going on and why. But just as Gone-in-the-Water had finished his pipe, a new figure appeared. He did not walk into the crowd but stood apart, his arms folded across his chest, the expression on his tattooed face stern. He was first noticed because of his priestly garb, but most of the people also knew him by name: Kanegwati, Water Moccasin. He was a young *kutani*, known to be close to Standing-in-the-Doorway. If the conjurer noticed the presence of the priest, he gave no indication.

Gone-in-the-Water refilled and relit his pipe. Then he handed it to Hemp Carrier, who took four puffs and handed it back. The pipe was thus passed to each of the six men and returned to the conjurer. Gone-in-the-Water then meticulously put away all of his things. When he was done, he stood facing the men.

"It's enough," he said. "Everything should go well. I suggest that you search the road which eventually leads to the Choctaw country. That's where you will find the three missing youngsters."

"Let's go then," shouted Hemp Carrier, and a general shout of encouragement arose from the crowd, but the strong voice of Water Moccasin rang clearly through the noise.

"*Hlesdi,*" he called out, effectively demanding a stop to all the noise and all the activity. The crowd was quiet. The six warriors and the mothers of the three children all looked toward the interfering priest. He stood for a moment in silence, then walked over to stand beside Gone-in-the-Water, facing the warriors. "What's happening here?" he said in a quiet voice. The Spoiler stepped out to confront him.

"Three of our children have been missing all night," she said. "These men are going to look for them."

"Is that all?" said the priest, his look adding that he knew that it was not.

"Yes," said the Spoiler. "That's all." But she knew that he knew the purpose of the ceremony, so she continued.

"We think maybe some Choctaws took them, so these men have been prepared in case they have to fight."

"That could lead to war," said Water Moccasin. "Do you have permission to go on this excursion?"

"There's no time," said the Spoiler. "It's our children."

"Nevertheless," said the priest, "these men cannot go. Not without the permission of Standing-in-the-Doorway."

"That will take time," said Wild Hemp. "They could be all the way into the country of the Choctaws by then."

"I have told you how it is," said Water Moccasin. "There are no exceptions."

Six

THE PRIEST WAS GONE, and the six men who had planned to go after the missing youngsters were standing near the gate of the city. Ready to go, they had been ordered not to go. They fidgeted, and they fumed. They felt foolish in front of the large crowd.

"But we've been made ready," said Stinging Ant.

"Is that a right of the *Ani-Kutani,*" asked Kick Up, "to say that we cannot go?"

No one answered immediately. Then the soft voice of an old man in the crowd imposed itself on the silence.

"There was a time when it was not," he said thoughtfully. "I remember. There was a time."

"I say let's go," said Hemp Carrier defiantly. "We've been properly prepared by Gone-in-the-Water, and the children may be in danger. We're wasting our time here with this argument."

"We can't go against the priests," said Big Bear.

"They are taking on too many powers," said Hemp Carrier. "Who says they can tell us not to go after our children when they are in trouble? Has anyone here ever heard of that before? Come on with me."

Hemp Carrier brandished his warclub, a carved, stylized red-bellied woodpecker, *dalala*, with its beak opened wide and its tongue protruding, and a copper celt driven through the gaping mouth to extend out the back of the head. The celt was perhaps half the length of the distance from Hemp Carrier's elbow to the tips of his fingers. He made a sound imitating the gobble of *guhna*, the wild turkey, and he headed toward the gate. The other men took up the war cry of the turkey with him and started to follow him.

"Wait," said the Spoiler. The men stopped, looking back toward her. "I don't know what's right and what's wrong," she said. "That's what the priests are there to tell us. But I know that if you go now, after Water Moccasin has been here to forbid it in the name of Standing-in-the-Doorway, there will be trouble for you."

"But what about our children?" said Wild Hemp.

"I'll go to War Woman," said the Spoiler, "the sister of Standing-in-the-Doorway. I'll ask her to bring her brother out of Men's Town to see me. We'll get his permission, and then the men can go."

"Time is wasting," said Agili.

"Then come with me," the Spoiler said. "I'll go to War Woman. From there we'll go to Men's Town and get the permission. You can then leave immediately from Men's Town and be on your way. Let's go now."

They left Ijodi, the mothers and the bristling war party. War Woman lived not far out of Men's Town in a small cluster of houses, hardly enough to call a town. As they walked, Hemp Carrier became more and more angry, more frustrated, and his sense of outrage grew. He and the others had been chastised in front of the entire population of Ijodi, in front of his neighbors and friends and relatives, as if they had been children. And they were not even being the aggressors here. They were not setting out to deliberately start a war with the Choctaws. If they were wrong about the Choctaws, if the children were simply lost or in some other kind of trouble, they would find them and bring them home and that would be the end of it. They had prepared for battle just in case their suspicions about the Choctaws proved to be true.

Most important of all in the mind of Hemp Carrier was the sense that the priests were preventing him from performing one of his most sacred duties. Hemp Carrier was the brother of Sparrow's mother, and that meant that Sparrow was his special charge. It was the duty of Hemp Carrier to teach, to discipline and to protect Sparrow. Now it looked as if Sparrow was in some kind of real trouble, and the priests were preventing Hemp Carrier from even going to look for the boy. Walking alone, thinking about these things, Hemp Carrier was furious.

They found War Woman at home. The most powerful, the most influential woman among the Real People, her son would be Standing-in-the-Doorway's successor one day. She was a tall woman, rawboned but shapely, still a striking beauty in her middle years. She had earned her name in her youth, and she knew and respected the Spoiler for having accomplished similar feats to her own. She welcomed the Spoiler and Wild Hemp to her house.

"How can I help you?" she said.

The Spoiler told War Woman about Sparrow, Corn Flower and Acorn, and she told her about her fears for their safety.

"Yes," said War Woman. "It is possible. The Choctaws were angry about the loss of the ball game and the disputed territory. They might have done something like that." She glanced over the Spoiler's shoulder at the six men who were waiting back there at a respectful distance. "What is this?" she said.

"They were going to look for the children," said the Spoiler. "They were prepared for battle by Gone-in-the-Water in case it really was the Choctaws. But Water Moccasin, a *kutani*, came, and he said they can't go without the permission of your brother."

War Woman looked at the men for a moment. Memories of old battles and of her own war honors stirred her blood.

"So what do you want of me?" she said.

"I've heard that Standing-in-the-Doorway sometimes refuses to even come out of Men's Town to talk to people. These men are ready to go now, and if the Choctaws really do have our children, they might get back to their own country before our men can catch them. Even now it may already be too late."

"I'll go with you to Men's Town," said War Woman. "My brother will come out for me. He will hear you."

The men stopped to wait maybe thirty paces away from the gate while the three women went ahead. Like-a-Pumpkin was standing on the ledge on the inside of the wall on watch. When he saw the women approaching the gate, he hurried down from his post and ran through the gateway to intercept them. They stopped outside the wall.

"Do you know me?" asked War Woman.

"Yes," said the priest. "Is there something I can do for you?"

"Tell Standing-in-the-Doorway that his sister is waiting at the gate."

"I'll tell him," said the priest, and he turned and ran

back through the gateway. War Woman glanced toward Wild Hemp and the Spoiler.

"He'll come," she said.

For a while, Hemp Carrier doubted that War Woman knew what she was talking about. Standing-in-the-Doorway, he thought, would make anybody wait, even his own sister, just to demonstrate his own importance. He asked himself just how long he would be able to wait, quietly enduring this humiliation. The arrogant priest, he thought, would probably not show himself at all. But he did.

Standing-in-the-Doorway stepped out, resplendent in his feathered capes. War Woman gestured to the other two women to stay where they were, a few paces to her left, and she stepped up close to her brother.

" 'Siyo, sister," said Standing-in-the-Doorway. "Are things well with you?"

"Yes. Well enough," War Woman said. "And with you?"

"Very well," said the priest. "So. What brings you to Men's Town? And who are these with you?"

"These people are from Ijodi, brother. They came to me for help. There are three young people who are missing. These two women are mothers of two of the children."

"And the men back there?"

"Uncle, a father and a brother."

"They seem to be dressed for war," said Standing-in-the-Doorway.

"Yes," War Woman said. "They are afraid that some Choctaws may have taken their children. The men were going to search for the children. They've prepared themselves for war in case they find the children captive."

Standing-in-the-Doorway paced away from War

Woman, his arms crossed over his chest, and he studied the men from a distance. Then he walked back to his sister.

"Yet they have not gone," he said.

"Your young priest Water Moccasin showed up and stopped them. He told them they had to have your permission. They might start a war with the Choctaws."

"That's true, of course," said Standing-in-the-Doorway. "We've only just now avoided a war with the Choctaws by settling a dispute by means of a ball play. The Choctaws were in a bad mood when they left here. It wouldn't take much from us to start a war with them. Water Moccasin was correct in what he said to these men."

"Because of that," said War Woman, "do we let the Choctaws insult us? Do we let them steal our children and do nothing about it because we are afraid that we might start a war?"

"Of course not," snapped Standing-in-the-Doorway. "But we have to consider these things carefully. A war could cost many lives. We don't rush into such a thing. We deliberate. We think and we plan. How old are these children?"

War Woman looked toward Wild Hemp and the Spoiler for the answer to Standing-in-the-Doorway's question.

"They will not be children much longer," said the Spoiler, "unless the Choctaws kill them. Then they will never be grown."

"I don't know," said Standing-in-the-Doorway. "I don't know. I should meet with my advisors." He faced his sister again. "Do you know these—young people?"

"No," she said, "I do not. But they are our people, Real People. They are our children."

"But you know them, Standing-in-the-Doorway," said the Spoiler, boldly approaching the priest. "They gave you squirrels."

The right eyebrow of Standing-in-the-Doorway rose slightly. "Their names?" he said.

"Sparrow, Corn Flower and Acorn," said the Spoiler.

Again the *kutani* paced away, seemingly deep in thought. Then he turned again to face the women. When he spoke again, it was in a loud, clear and authoritative voice.

"My sister is a wise woman," he said. "There is no need to consult with other advisors. Our children are important to us. It is also important that the Choctaws know that we will not allow them or anyone else to insult the Real People and go unpunished." He paused a moment, then raised his voice a little more, looking toward the waiting men. "You have my permission," he said. "Go."

They took the path that led from Men's Town back to the big road, the road that wound by Ijodi and to Kituwah and eventually ran all the way into the country of the Choctaw people. Hemp Carrier led the way, trying to clear his mind of the anger and bitterness it held toward Standing-in-the-Doorway, telling himself that all of his attention was required to find the youngsters, to keep from blundering into a Choctaw trap. The safety of his nephew depended on it, and the safety of the others. But the arrogance of the *kutani* was almost too much to put up with. To even suggest that men of the Real People could not set out in search of their own missing children, could not perform their most sacred duties and responsibilities without first humbling themselves before a *kutani*, was infuriating.

He called a sudden halt.

"Agili," he said, "have you seen any sign on the road to tell us that they've been by this way? My mind has been distracted by thoughts of the priests."

"The road here has been too well traveled lately," said Agili. "One cannot tell. Maybe farther out we'll find some sign."

"All we can do then," said Hemp Carrier, "is to keep going on this road. We have to assume that they've been captured by the Choctaws."

So they kept to the road. If the priests had not held them up so long, thought Hemp Carrier, they would be much farther along their way. The day was already almost half gone, almost half wasted chasing after priests.

It was late in the evening when Agili saw the first sign. It was a clear footprint in soft ground near the edge of the road, so clear that he could see the imprint of the stitching which outlined the sole of the moccasin.

"Look," he said. "That is my sister's work. This print was made by Corn Flower. She has been here—maybe this time yesterday."

"Then the others were probably here, too," said Hemp Carrier. He looked around, and so did the others, but they found no clear sign. "They are maybe one day ahead of us then," he said, "but soon it will be dark. We'll have to camp here. In the morning, as soon as there's light, we'll start again."

Seven

IT WAS MORNING AGAIN. The Choctaws, after having slept half a day, had traveled the rest of that day, then camped for the night. Sparrow had followed, waiting for the right opportunity. He chastised himself for having waited so long. The changed pattern of their traveling indicated to him that they now felt safe. He did not know where he was or how far away from home he had traveled. For all he knew, they were already in the homeland of the Choctaws. Perhaps, he thought, he had not really been waiting for the right opportunity. Perhaps he had simply been delaying any action because he was afraid. His chances had probably been better earlier. He did not like the thought that he might have been behaving in a cowardly manner.

He had not had a good meal since leaving Ijodi, and the Choctaws had been eating well. He told himself he would have to act soon, yet he did not know what to do. The Choctaws were awake again. He had allowed yet another chance to sneak into their camp to go by, had wasted yet another opportunity. He told himself that he could not just rush in and attack them. That would almost certainly just get him killed and do no good whatsoever for his friends. As before, the Choctaws had made their camp just at the side of the road, and, as before, Sparrow lurked in the woods on the opposite side of the road from the camp.

He had awakened in a panic, afraid that he had slept too long, afraid that his quarry would be long gone. But they were still there, and they did not seem to be in a hurry to get started. Sparrow thought again, they must be close to home. They were relaxed, talking and laughing. Now and then one or two or all of them glanced toward Corn Flower. Sparrow wondered what they were waiting for. Why didn't they get started? Then one of the Choctaws walked over close to Corn Flower, but one of his comrades spoke sharply. He stopped and turned, facing back toward the other two, and right away all three seemed to be arguing. Sparrow wasn't sure why, but he picked up his blowgun and tucked a dart into one end.

The argument seemed to be resolved almost as suddenly as it had begun, and one of the men peeled off his breechclout and dropped it to the ground. Even from where he hid, Sparrow could see the evidence of the man's arousal as he moved slowly and menacingly toward Corn Flower.

"Get away," Corn Flower shouted.

The two watching men laughed as Corn Flower scooted on the ground backward, away from her stalker. A few feet away, Acorn cowered and trembled, his wide eyes fixed on the naked man who was threatening his companion. The naked man spoke harshly, bent forward and grabbed Corn Flower by an ankle. She kicked and twisted on the ground, shouting at the man to leave her alone. Sparrow acted on a sudden impulse. Without thinking, he brought the blowgun to his lips, aimed, filled his lungs and cheeks with air and gave a mighty, explosive puff. The sharp honey locust dart sped through the air to bury about a third of its length in the naked left cheek of the man's buttocks, causing him to shriek in pain and surprise. First he slapped at his own rump, as if he had been stung by a giant wasp. Then, recognizing the truth, he grabbed for the offending missile. Acorn and Corn Flower shot each other a glance.

"Tsisquaya," Corn Flower whispered. "It's Sparrow."

The wounded man was engaged in an attempt to extract the vicious dart from his flesh, alternately groaning and howling with pain, while his two comrades frantically looked around, searching the surrounding fringes of the forest for signs of their surprise attacker. Then Panther estimated the angle and the trajectory of the dart and pointed in the general direction of Sparrow's hiding place. He said something to Crawling Snake, the wounded man, as he grabbed up his own weapons, and he spoke sharply to Fox Skin, the other, who had also armed himself by then.

Sparrow was poised for action, but he didn't know what kind of action it would be. He was confused and frightened. He had temporarily saved the situation only to create a new one. If he stayed where he was, they would surely find him. The two Choctaws were moving in his direction, one on each side of the road. Corn Flower had scrambled to her feet, and Sparrow saw the naked man with the wounded cheek push her back to the ground. The other two were getting closer. Sparrow could easily turn and escape into the woods, but he wanted to keep these men away from his friends for a time, to keep their minds from turning back to their previous lustful intentions. He inserted another dart into his blowgun and stood up, exposing the upper half of his body to the view of the Choctaws, and he quickly fired the missile.

"Ahh," Panther shouted.

The dart had stabbed into the soft flesh just under his left clavicle. He shouted a command to Fox Skin, pointing at Sparrow. Sparrow stepped out into the road.

"You are vomit-eating dogs," he shouted, hoping that the Choctaws would at least understand by his tone that they had been insulted, and then he turned and started to run back down the road, back the way they had already traveled. Fox Skin, the one unhurt Choctaw, ran after him. Panther plucked out the dart with a sharp cry of pain and anger and threw it to the ground. Then he, too, began to run after Sparrow.

Back in the camp the naked Crawling Snake had looked in the direction of the chase when he heard Panther's shout, and as he did, Corn Flower, still on the ground, swung her powerful long legs in a wide arc, striking him just behind the knees. His legs buckled, and he fell hard on his back. She scampered to her feet, shouting.

"Get up, Acorn. Run."

She kicked again, this time delivering a hard blow to the side of the fallen man's head. Acorn was by then on his feet.

"Come on," said Corn Flower, and she turned and ran, leading the frightened Acorn into the forest. The running was difficult with their hands tied behind them. Twice Acorn stumbled and fell, and each time he did, Corn Flower stopped to wait for him. "Get up," she said. "If they catch us now, they'll kill us." She ran on until Acorn thought that his lungs would burst, and then, at last, she stopped. "Wait," she said, and she listened to the sounds of the forest until she was satisfied. "No one is following us, I think," she said. "They must be after Sparrow. Except the one I kicked. I think I broke his jaw. We have to get our hands loose now and look for Sparrow. Come on. He may need our help."

Just then, Acorn burst into tears and convulsive sobs.

Sparrow ran. He glanced over his shoulder, and he saw that the one back there was getting closer. He had to make another decision or he would be caught. He fumbled with the blowgun as he ran, pulling loose another dart and loading it into the gun. It slowed him down to do this, he knew. The man would be even closer, but that would be all right. He would not be able to get the breath for a long shot. As quickly as he could, he stopped and turned. The man was close. A few more long strides would bring him crashing into Sparrow. Sparrow fired. The dart, at such close range, was driven into the man's stomach clear up to its tuft of down. The man doubled over in pain and tumbled in the road. Sparrow turned and ran off the side of the road into the woods.

"Look," said Agili, pointing ahead. He had already found the tracks leading off the road and up onto the ridge, and, following those, he had seen the two abandoned blowguns. He hurried ahead, the others following. Agili picked up the two blowguns and examined them. "This belongs to Corn Flower," he said. He handed the other to Hemp Carrier.

"This must be Acorn's weapon," Hemp Carrier said. "It is not the one I made for my nephew."

"But there should be three," said Stinging Ant.

"Wait," said Agili. He began looking carefully around, studying the ground, looking at mashed blades of grass, broken twigs, bent branches of brush, overturned rocks, looking for whatever he might find. The others looked, too, but mostly they waited for Agili. He was the best at this tracking and reading of sign. At last he stood up and pointed along the ridge. "They continued along this way, I think," he said. "All but one. One went over the edge right here."

"Which one?" asked Hemp Carrier.

"I don't know which one. I'll go down and look. I think the rest of you should keep going along this ridge. I think it will take you back down to the road somewhere up ahead. When I have seen all I can see down there, I'll go back to the road and catch up with you."

"*Howa*," said Hemp Carrier, indicating his agreement. "Let's go."

The others followed him along the ridge as Agili began his cautious descent of the steep hillside. It was a difficult path he had chosen, and once he nearly fell, but eventually he found the brush and boulders which had finally broken the fall of Sparrow. He still did not know who had fallen, but he felt almost certain that it had been one of the three young people. Then he found the thongs which had bound Sparrow's wrists. He picked them up to take along with him. He studied the surrounding area some more, and he noticed that up above, small saplings and tough clumps of grass showed signs of having been pulled on hard from downhill. Whoever had fallen, he decided, had climbed back up again. Had that person climbed back up before the others had left or after? He could not tell. When he was at last convinced that he could learn no more, he worked his way on down to the road and raced ahead to join the others. He caught up with them just as they reached the road.

"What did you find?" said Hemp Carrier.

"Whoever fell down the hill climbed back up," said Agili. "That's all I could tell."

"Then they're all still together," said Stinging Ant.

"Maybe," said Agili. "Maybe not. Where the fall stopped, a person could hide from anyone up on the ridge. Maybe the others left, and then that one climbed back up. I don't know. Except I found these."

He held out the thongs to show the others.

"It looks like someone's wrists were bound with these," said Stinging Ant.

"And they've been cut," said Big Bear.

"Sparrow's blowgun is missing," said Hemp Carrier. "Maybe it was Sparrow who went down and hid. Then when the others left, maybe he freed himself, climbed back up, got his weapon and followed them."

"It could have happened like that," said Agili. "If he fell with his hands tied, the Choctaws probably thought that he was badly hurt and not worth going after. That's why they left him there."

"We'd better hurry," said Big Bear, "before something else happens."

"Yes," said Hemp Carrier. "If it hasn't already. Come on."

As they moved on, Hemp Carrier felt a renewed sense of urgency. The discarded bonds seemed to confirm the already strong suspicion that the youngsters had been captured, probably by disgruntled Choctaws. And he thought again of the arrogance of Standing-in-the-Door-way and the critical time the priest had caused them to waste.

Eight

SPARROW SAT DOWN exhausted and leaned back against a large tree trunk to catch his breath. The serenity of the woods around him was disturbed, it seemed, only by his presence. Overhead two jays scolded him. He knew that he was safe from any pursuit, at least for a time. The Choctaw who had been nearest to him had taken the dart in the belly at fairly close range. It had gone in deep, and the wound, Sparrow thought, must be extremely painful. The men were in no real danger from the darts, unless one struck an eye or maybe a soft temple, but the tiny wounds would hurt. Now, however, Sparrow realized, he had a real problem. The men knew he was out there. They would be watching for him, and since all three of them had been stung by his darts, they would be angry and vengeful. He hoped that they would not take that anger out on Corn Flower and Acorn. He also worried that they might now hurry on with their captives to their nearest town. He wondered how far that might be.

He knew that his chances of rescuing his friends had

been better before he had exposed himself, but still, he thought, he had not really had any other choice. Had he not fired that first dart, the man would have had his way with Corn Flower, perhaps all three men. That thought almost sickened Sparrow with revulsion, and he wished that he had been able to cause more harm to the hated Choctaws. If he had only had a bow and some arrows, he would have killed the man. He would have killed all three. Sparrow longed to be a man and to carry the weapons of a man. He held up his blowgun and looked at it with scorn. A child's weapon. But almost immediately he relented. It had, after all, served him well.

He was breathing evenly again, and he tried to get his mind back on business. He would have to work his way carefully back to a position where he could continue to spy on the Choctaws, to watch for an opportunity to save his friends. He thought that the men were probably back in their camp nursing their wounds, but he wondered if they would be angry enough to pursue him again, or if they would now be in a hurry to get safely home with their two captives. He decided to wait a little longer to try to determine whether or not they were looking for him. If they were not, then surely they would be headed for their home.

"Turn around this way," said Corn Flower. "I'll try to get your hands loose."

They stood back to back with Corn Flower fumbling at the knots which bound Acorn's wrists together. The knots were tight and she couldn't see what she was doing. In addition, her own fingers were numb because of her own bonds.

"Hurry up," said Acorn.

"I can't get them," she said. "See if you can undo mine."

"They'll be coming after us," said Acorn, a desperate whine in his voice.

"One of them won't," she said, recalling with pleasant satisfaction the kick she had delivered to her would-be attacker's jaw. "We have some time. Come on. See if you can untie me."

Acorn felt for the knot, his fingers pulling here and there.

"Oh," he said. "I can't— Wait. Wait. I've got it. Be still. I think I'm getting it now."

Soon he had it untied. Corn Flower pulled the loosened thongs from her wrists and threw them to the ground. She shook her wrists to get the blood circulating normally through her hands once again. Acorn hopped up and down nervously.

"Get mine now," he said. "Undo me. Hurry."

"All right. Be still then," she said, and she got him untied. "There."

"Do you know the way home?" he asked.

"Yes, but we're not going home. We have to find Sparrow."

"Why?" said Acorn. "Sparrow can take care of himself. Let's go home. I'm hungry and tired, and I'm afraid."

"Go, then," she said.

"I can't go by myself. I can't find the way alone."

"Then stay with me. We're going to find Sparrow."

"How can we find him? We don't know where he went."

"He ran straight down the road," said Corn Flower. "He won't be hard to find. Now, let's go."

She stayed hidden in the trees, but she moved closer to the road again and began walking in a line parallel to the road. The last she had seen of Sparrow, he had been standing in the middle of the road. He had just shot the second Choctaw, and another was still running after him. She had then sprung into action and had not had time to watch Sparrow anymore. He might still be running down the road with the last Choctaw chasing him. He might be back in the woods. But he was somewhere up ahead, and she would find him.

Hemp Carrier was convinced that there would be a battle with the Choctaws. He and his companions were still on the road, and they had gone far enough that they knew they could only be headed for the country of the Choctaws. Agili had seen more sign along the way, and he was certain that there were at least three Choctaw men, and that they had Corn Flower and Acorn captive. He had seen no sign of Sparrow since the place where Sparrow had fallen down the steep hillside. Up ahead a small creek ran across the road. Agili was in the lead, and he stopped, looking at the soft, wet ground.

"*Ni,*" he said. "Look. This is where Sparrow walked, and he came along after the others."

"Then it's just as we thought," said Hemp Carrier. "He's free, and he's following them. He means to rescue his friends."

Big Bear looked worried.

"He can't fight three grown men by himself," he said. "He's still a boy."

"But he will try," said Hemp Carrier, "if we don't catch up to them first. Come on. Let's hurry."

Fox Skin, with the stomach wound, was stretched out on the ground at the site where the Choctaws had last made camp, while Panther examined his wound. It was a small puncture, like the others, but it was deep, as deep as the length of a man's forefinger maybe. Panther looked at the dart which had done the damage.

"It's good you have so much fat on your belly," he said, "otherwise even this small projectile could have done serious damage to your insides."

"Ah." Fox Skin winced in pain. "It must have done serious damage. It hurts."

"It's a dart for killing birds," said Panther. He pinched a chunk of Fox Skin's belly around the wound and squeezed it. "And it did not get through your belly fat. You'll be just fine."

"It's not as bad as mine," said Crawling Snake, the still naked one. "Mine makes me limp like a cripple. I can't sit down. And I think that my jaw may be broken."

He carefully put a hand to his swollen jaw. His puffy face was beginning to discolor there where Corn Flower had kicked him. Panther stood up and paced out into the middle of the road, staring off in the direction of Sparrow's escape.

"I thought that we were going home with some captive *Chalakee* children," he said, "but they have escaped, and you two are acting more like children than they."

"Let's catch them and kill them," said Fox Skin.

"I don't want to kill them right away," said Crawling Snake. "At least, not the girl. But we can kill her later if you like. I won't care then."

"We're not going to kill them," said Panther. "We're not even going to chase them. We're not going to do anything more, except go home."

Crawling Snake hobbled toward Panther, an expression of disbelief on his disfigured face.

"How can you say that?" he said. "How could we do that? We would have to admit that three children,

Chalakee children, escaped from us, wounded us with their toys, and we did nothing. That would be dishonorable."

"No," said Panther. "It was dishonorable for us to capture the children in the first place. We had a bargain with the *Chalakees*. The ball game would settle the dispute. We lost. But we three were poor losers. We acted in anger and on impulse. We were wrong. Now they have escaped, and no one has been hurt—much. Let's go home."

"But our wounds," said Crawling Snake.

"If we keep quiet about them," said Panther, "maybe no one will ask anything. Players are always battered up after a ball game." He reached down with his long warclub and scooped the neglected breechclout up from the ground, then held it out toward its owner. "Here," he said. "Cover yourself. You look foolish."

Sparrow sat up stiff and alert. He could hear someone approaching through the woods from the direction of the Choctaws' camp. At least two, he thought. He stood up slowly, blowgun in hand. Should he run again? He was tired of running. He wanted this thing to be over and done. He wanted his friends to be free and back with him, and he wanted them all three to be back home in Ijodi. He put a dart in the blowgun, deciding to stand his ground. Besides the one he had just loaded, there were only two more darts. He would have to be more deadly with the darts, he thought. Aim for the eyes. The small puncture wounds in the flesh of big, angry men were almost useless.

He listened. The noise was louder. Whoever it was coming through the woods was closer and still moving in his direction. He slipped around behind the tree for cover and waited. Then he heard voices.

"Corn Flower, let's go back to the road."

"Go anywhere you want to. I'm going this way."

Sparrow stepped out from behind the tree.

"Corn Flower!" he shouted. "Acorn. It's me. Sparrow. I'm here."

"Sparrow," Corn Flower called, and then she ran ahead toward his voice. Acorn ran behind her. As they came into view, Sparrow ran to meet them.

"You got free," he said. "How did you do it?"

"When you shot that man," said Corn Flower, "the other two chased you. That left only one with us. He was watching you and the others, and I kicked him, and we ran. In the woods we untied each other. But there were two of them chasing you. How did you get away?"

"I shot them both," said Sparrow. "I guess it hurt them enough to slow them down, and I ran in here."

"Do you think they're still looking for us?" asked Acorn.

"I don't know," said Sparrow. "Let's go home, but let's watch over our shoulders until we know that we're safe."

Nine

"THREE CHOCTAWS," said Hemp Carrier, "and all of them hurt."

The rescue party had met the young people on the road, and they had heard the whole story. Agili's skill as a tracker was praised, for all of his surmises had been borne out by the story the youngsters told. Acorn complained bitterly that he was tired and hungry.

"I think only two of us need to follow the Choctaws," said Hemp Carrier. "Big Bear and I will go after them. The rest of you go with the—young people back to Ijodi."

He almost said "children," but he had corrected himself in time. Sparrow and Corn Flower, at least, had certainly not behaved like children.

"Uncle," said Sparrow, "let me go with you."

Hemp Carrier looked at his nephew, his sister's son, the child it had been his role to train in the ways of a hunter and a warrior, to praise and to punish, depending on the situation. He put a hand on Sparrow's shoulder.

"You've done well, nephew," he said. "Now I think you

should go home. Let me and your father finish off these Choctaws for you."

Big Bear and Hemp Carrier found the last campsite of the Choctaws with no trouble, and they examined it carefully. They agreed that all three Choctaws seemed to have given up on their captives and headed home.

"Perhaps they were too badly hurt to pursue our youngsters," said Hemp Carrier.

"Two of them might have been," agreed Big Bear. "Corn Flower said that her kick could have broken the jaw of the one."

"Yes. And Sparrow shot another one in the belly. Even a small dart could be harmful there."

"So. Shall we follow them farther?"

"For a little ways," said Hemp Carrier. "Enough to be sure that they have really given up and gone home. Then, I think, we can forget them."

"I agree," said Big Bear. "It should be enough, what Corn Flower and Sparrow have done to them."

Hemp Carrier chuckled, thinking about the action that had been described to them earlier.

"Yes," he said. "It should be."

There was much rejoicing in Ijodi when the three youngsters returned. Their mothers hugged them and looked them over to make sure they were unhurt, and then they began to feed them. Their friends and neighbors and relatives brought them food, too, and soon the whole town was involved in a great impromptu celebration. Soon the activities had progressed to the townhouse plaza. All three youngsters were enjoying the attention and the general festive air. This had not been going on for long when Hemp Carrier and Big Bear returned. The crowd grew quiet in anticipation, for they knew already that these two men had gone on in pursuit of the kidnappers.

"Tell us what happened," someone said. "Did you kill them?"

"No," said Hemp Carrier. "When we found their camp, they had already gone home. These three had escaped from them, beaten them and chased them away, all without our help."

"We should go into one of their towns and get revenge for what they've done," said another.

"We don't have to do that," said Hemp Carrier. "You haven't yet heard, I guess, just how badly our brave young people humiliated those three."

Then an old woman stepped forward and suggested that they all move inside the large townhouse and let the youngsters tell their tale. If they had behaved like warriors, then they should be treated as such at home. Everyone agreed, and soon the people were all inside. The seven-sided townhouse, or council house, was the center of Ijodi. It sat atop a man-made mound of earth and had been constructed much like the smaller family dwellings of the town. The walls were made of small logs, daubed with mud. The roof was dome-shaped. Inside, tiered benches lined the walls, and a perpetual fire burned in a central altar.

Each of the seven clans had its designated seating area, and soon all of the people had taken their proper places. Sparrow was pushed to the center of the floor to speak. He felt his heart pounding in his chest, and his knees began to shake. He had never before been in such a situation, and he had not expected it to happen to him on this occasion. He had always assumed that someday, when he was a man, he would speak before all the people, but this had come so suddenly that he was unprepared. Hemp

Carrier noted his nephew's hesitation, and he understood it.

"Just tell us all what happened," he said. "How were you captured?"

"We were just out walking," said Sparrow, "between Ijodi and Kituwah, my friends and I. Corn Flower and Acorn and I. And three Choctaws came out of the woods. They were ball players. I recognized them from the ball play. They had warclubs, and they threatened us. We didn't know what to do, and they tied our hands and took us with them."

Sparrow paused, and there were low murmurs from the crowd, murmurs about the devious Choctaws. Sparrow's knees continued to shake, and he wondered if everyone could see them doing that. He tried tightening his leg muscles, but he couldn't stop the shaking. The murmurs subsided, and he continued his tale.

"We walked with them for a long way. They had left the road, I guess so they wouldn't be seen. They were taking us around Kituwah, and we wound up on a high ridge. They stopped to rest, and I yelled for my uncle, Hemp Carrier. I didn't think he was anywhere around, but I thought it might make the Choctaws worry. One of them swung his ax at me, and I fell down the side. I went way down, a long way, and I stopped sliding in some bushes, and I was hidden by the bushes and by some boulders. I just kept real still, and they went on. So I got my hands loose, and I followed them."

Corn Flower stepped up beside Sparrow. She was excited and did not seem nervous at all about standing there in front of the whole town.

"We were afraid that Sparrow had been killed," she said. "It was a long way down there, and we couldn't see him. Then they took us farther and farther from home. I wondered if we would ever get back. I wondered what they would do to us, and I worried about Sparrow. Then when the Choctaws had made a camp, Acorn and I still had our hands tied behind us, and we were on the ground. One of the Choctaws uncovered himself. He was completely naked, and he came after me."

There were audible gasps from the crowd. Corn Flower was becoming more animated. Her eyes were opened wide as she continued her story.

"He came for me, with his tool standing straight out. I backed away from him, and I shouted at him. 'Get away from me,' I said. But he kept coming, and he reached for me and grabbed me by my leg. I kicked and screamed, and just then, he let me go. He shrieked out. He jumped, and he slapped at his bare rear end."

Here Corn Flower imitated the actions of the man, much to the delight of her audience. She hopped and she slapped herself, twisting this way and that.

"Then I saw it. Sticking in him just there. It was a dart. I looked down the road, and there was Sparrow with his blowgun."

The crowd laughed uproariously. Like a polished story-teller, Corn Flower waited for the laughter to begin to subside before continuing.

"The Choctaws saw him, too, and they ran after him. All but the naked one with the wounded rump."

Again her audience laughed. Sparrow marveled at her abilities and her bold confidence, but he realized again that he was watching her and listening to her with something more than friendship, more even than admiration. These thoughts troubled him, but he also noticed that his knees had stopped shaking.

"The naked man watched his two friends chase Sparrow," she said, "and he turned his back to me, so I knew it was time to act. I kicked his legs out from under him, and he fell down hard on his back. I got up as fast as I could, and I kicked him again. I kicked him in the side of his head, and I think I broke his jaw with that one. Then Acorn and I ran into the woods. We untied each other and started to look for Sparrow."

She stopped and gave Sparrow a look, as if to say, "It's your turn now. Finish the story." Sparrow hesitated only a moment.

"I ran," he said, "but I still had my blowgun. One man was closer to me than the other, so I turned and shot him. I hit him just here."

Sounds of approval came from the crowd as Sparrow touched himself just below the left clavicle. He started to speak again, but at that moment, he noticed Acorn sitting in the front row of the Bird Clan section of the house, a dark frown on his face, and he saw from Acorn's point of view what was happening. Sparrow and Corn Flower were being treated like heroes. They were getting all the glory. Acorn was left out entirely. He tried to tell himself that if Acorn wanted glory, he should behave differently, and he went on with his story.

"I ran on a little more," he said, his manner somewhat subdued, "and then I turned once again and fired another dart. This one hit the third Choctaw in his belly. He fell over, and I ran on into the woods then. Pretty soon Corn Flower and Acorn found me. We started for home and met my uncle and the others along the way. That's all."

He walked over to take a seat beside Acorn, and as he turned to sit down, he saw, just inside the entrance and flanked by four lesser priests, Standing-in-the-Doorway. How long, he wondered, had they been there? Then he saw, even from across the room, that the eyes of Standing-in-the-Doorway were fixed on Acorn. There was some more talking, but Sparrow didn't hear it. He felt a cold sensation, something akin to fear, and it had something vague to do with Standing-in-the-Doorway and with Acorn. At the same time, his mind was still struggling trying to come to grips with his feelings for Corn Flower. When he was next aware of what was happening around him, the young pumpkin-faced priest was addressing the crowd.

"Standing-in-the-Doorway commends the people of Ijodi for the way in which they handled this tense and potentially dangerous situation," he said. "He especially applauds the bravery of these three young people, and, as a special way of honoring this community, he has chosen this opportunity to announce his selection of the young man Acorn as apprentice priest."

Acorn sat up straight, his wide eyes staring across the room at Standing-in-the-Doorway. Did I hear right? he asked himself. Did he say my name? He glanced around, and it seemed that all eyes were turned toward him. He had heard right. He must have. Acorn. A *kutani*. Then Standing-in-the-Doorway was gone, and so were the other priests, all except Like-a-Pumpkin, who was walking over toward Acorn.

"You've just received a great honor," he said. "Does it please you?"

"Yes," said Acorn, almost breathless. His heart raced, and he was trembling all over.

"You are to be at Men's Town in four days," said the *kutani*. "I'll be watching for you at the entrance."

Then he left, and Acorn felt puffed up. Sparrow and Corn Flower had gotten all the attention from the town, and Acorn had been left out. But Standing-in-the-Doorway's surprise announcement had changed all that. That's what they get, he thought. It serves them right. Does it please me? Yes. It pleases me. It pleases me greatly. It pleases me more than anything else could please me.

Sparrow saw the look on Acorn's face, and it frightened him a little. He also recalled the way Standing-in-the-Doorway always looked at Acorn. He could not have told anyone why he felt the way he did, but he felt certain that no good would come of this. He shot a glance toward Corn Flower. He could not read her face, yet that quick glance was enough to dispel a little of the sense of gloom that had embraced him, for it brought back to mind the confusion and anxiety of his new and still ambiguous feelings for her.

"Ah," he said quietly to himself, "she is truly amazing. Truly she is."

Ten

FOR A WHILE after Acorn left Ijodi to take up a new residence at Men's Town, Sparrow missed his old companion, in spite of Acorn's poutiness. He spent some time after that with Corn Flower, but it just wasn't the same as it had been when the three of them had been childhood companions. Acorn was gone, and Sparrow had a vague feeling that their last adventure together had somehow wrought a permanent change in Acorn. Perhaps, he thought, he is becoming a man. He hoped so. Sparrow's feelings toward Corn Flower had changed, too. He no longer enjoyed childish play with her, as if she were another boy. His feelings were confusing, and so he began to spend more and more time alone. The best excuse for getting out of Ijodi alone was hunting, and so Sparrow became a hunter. Gradually his hunts took him farther away from home and kept him away longer. The first time his mother expressed concern to him about his new habits, he thought about the story of the bears again, and it made him chuckle.

Still he stayed away more than he stayed at home, and his reputation as a hunter began to grow. People expected to see him return from his forays successful, bringing back fresh kills, and they were seldom disappointed. Eventually he earned for himself a new name. They called him Edohi, He-Is-Going-About. It was a little bit of a joke, because that was what he was always doing, but for the same reason, it was a serious and honorable name, and it made him proud. And then Sparrow, now Edohi, realized another thing. His new name was a man's name. He had thrown away his childhood with his child's name. He was Edohi, and he was a man.

It was just and it was proper. It was the way of the world. Time passed, and children grew into adults. Perhaps that was the whole reason for his confusion over the past few years since Acorn had gone away. And Acorn, too, had a new name. Edohi had not seen Acorn, but he had heard the news. The boy Acorn had become the man Two Heads, an apprentice priest, a *kutani*. It was said Two Heads was rapidly becoming the right-hand man of Standing-in-the-Doorway himself. Edohi did not like to think about Two Heads. He even had great difficulty pronouncing or even thinking the new name. He still thought of his old friend as Acorn.

He arrived at the grazing area. It was not far from Ijodi, yet not too close either. The people had cleared the land by girdling the trees, removing a ring of bark from around each trunk, close to the ground and then waiting for them to die. Then in the winter with the trees dead, they had burned the area to clear it. The resulting bed of ashes had fed the soil, and the field with its lush new growth attracted the deer. There were other methods of hunting, but on this day, Edohi had chosen to visit the browsing field to seek his prey. The grass looked dry, and he wondered if he had made the right choice. Well, he would see. He carried his long bow made of ash and strung with strips of buckskin tightly twisted together. He had six arrows made of the small, straight river cane and tipped with flint.

The previous night, Edohi had gone to the river and prayed to Long Man and to the Sacred Fire. He had begged their assistance, prayed for good dreams and for success in hunting. Then before going to sleep that night, he had rubbed his chest with ashes from the Sacred Fire which burned perpetually in Ijodi's townhouse. He had done everything as it should be done before a hunt, and so he was rewarded. He saw them there in the open field, five of them. One was a large male, and Edohi decided that was the one. He nocked an arrow, and very quietly he spoke the words intended to send it to its mark. Then he released it, and its flight was true and deadly. The buck flinched at the impact, ran forward a few steps, then fell over on one side to move no more. The other four animals, frightened and confused, ran for the safety and security of the deep woods. Edohi walked over to his kill.

He knelt beside the slain animal and addressed a short prayer to Awi-Usdi, Little Deer, the spirit chief of all deer. It was a prayer of thanks and of apology, and as he said the words, Edohi recalled the old story.

They said that in some long-ago time, a time just after people had acquired weapons and learned their use, the people were killing too many animals. It was so easy to kill with the new weapons, and the people showed no mercy. The animal tribes began to fear that they would soon be wiped out, and they had a big council to discuss this new problem.

"People are killing too many of us," someone said. "We have to do something about it."

"But what can we do?" said another.

"They are killing us with bows and arrows," said Yona, the Bear. "Let's get ourselves some bows and arrows and kill them."

And from somewhere, Yona got a bow and some arrows, but when he tried to nock the arrow and pull the string, his long, sharp claws got in the way. He was too clumsy, and the arrow just fell to the ground at his feet. Some of the others laughed, and Yona got mad and left the meeting.

It was Awi-Usdi then, Little Deer, who came up with the plan they adopted.

"We know," he said, "that people need to kill us for our flesh to eat. That is how they stay alive. But they should not kill more than what they need, and when they kill, they should show some respect and gratitude for what we give."

The others all agreed.

"So the hunter should go to the water and pray the night before he hunts. He should sleep the night beneath the Sacred Fire, and in the morning, he should not eat. Then before he shoots, he should say a prayer, and if his shot is true, he should then apologize for his need to kill. If he does all this, then everything will be all right."

"But," someone asked, "how can we make the people behave in such a way?"

"From now on," said Awi-Usdi, "anytime a human kills a deer, I will be there, and I'll watch and listen, and if the hunter fails to beg my pardon for what he's done, I'll heat him up from inside and make him sweat and cause his joints to swell."

The other animals laughed and cheered. It seemed to

all of them to be a great idea. Their imaginations went gleefully wild, and in turn each animal spirit chief dreamed up a new torment to inflict upon the wretched human who failed to show the proper attitude after having killed one of its kind.

The plant spirits overheard this council, and they began to take pity on the humans, so horrible were the forms of revenge invented by the animals. Each plant, therefore, determined to serve as an antidote for one of the vile torments devised by the animals. Thus the Real People explained the origin of both disease and medicine, and because of that, Edohi had properly performed all the prescribed rites of a hunter. Even so, just to be safe, he stopped four times on his way back to Ijodi to build small fires in the road on top of his own footprints. If Awi-Usdi followed him, the fire would throw him off the trail.

The fires were easy to make, because everything was dry, and Edohi took care each time to keep the fires very small and in the middle of the road. A long time had passed since the last rain. Water no longer flowed through several old, familiar mountain streams. Even the river was low, and all the land was dry and thirsty. Overhead the sun was hot. The sky was blue and clear. Edohi wondered how much longer they would have to wait for rain.

Standing-in-the-Doorway, too, worried about the rain. He worried for the same reasons that Edohi worried. Without rain, the life of the land was threatened. Plants dried up and died of thirst. The animals would move away from their accustomed places to look for water elsewhere. Gardens produced feeble plants or none. If the river levels dropped too low, whole towns might have to move. For all these reasons all the people worried about the rain, and all the people prayed for rain.

But Standing-in-the-Doorway worried more. He was the head man of the *Ani-Kutani*, the chief of all the priests. He had more power and more authority than anyone among the Real People, but he also had more responsibility. If the rain did not come soon, he would be blamed. He was the supreme spiritual leader of his people, with all the major religious ceremonies in his charge. It was on his head, and no one knew it more than he.

He stood in the doorway to a private room in the temple atop the great mound in the center of Men's Town, and he stared at the empty sky. It was bright blue and clear. There was no cloud to be seen in any direction. The sun was high and bright and hot. There was no sign of any kind that rain would be forthcoming. Standing-in-the-Doorway had already prayed for rain, both publicly and alone in secret. He had also conducted the appropriate public ceremonies. He was experiencing a quiet and private desperation. His reputation, and therefore his position, was in jeopardy.

He leaned back against the wall and slowly turned to face back into the room. It was dark inside, especially after he had stared so long and hard against the unrelenting brightness of the sky. But he knew the room intimately. He knew every corner of the room and every object in it. And he was looking toward the cot which stood against the far wall, the cot on which still slept the young priest Two Heads, the one who had been Acorn. Slowly the eyes of Standing-in-the-Doorway readjusted to the darkness of the room, and slowly the smooth and naked form of the young man came back into his view. Yes, he thought, he had so much to lose.

He considered waking Two Heads up, but he decided to wait, to let him sleep some more. He liked watching Two Heads sleep. He could stand there, he thought, just watching for a good long while. He could do that and feel so peaceful, if it were not for the troubles that weighed so heavily on his head. Something would have to be done about the troubles. He would have to find a way to bring the rain. Almost everything had been tried already, and now he knew that desperate measures were called for. There was much too much to lose.

Two Heads murmured, coming out of sleep. He rolled over on his back, then slowly sat up, rubbing his eyes. He looked across the room at Standing-in-the-Doorway framed there before the brightness of the sky.

"Have you been up long?" he asked.

"No," said Standing-in-the-Doorway. "Just for a little while."

"I'm sorry if I slept too long," said Two Heads. "Why didn't you wake me?"

"There was no need. I was watching you sleep. It gives me pleasure to watch you in your sleep."

Two Heads stood up and moved slowly toward Standing-in-the-Doorway. He stopped just by the head priest, almost touching him. Standing-in-the-Doorway put an arm around the bare shoulders and held the young man close.

"Look out there," he said. "There's no sign of rain. No hint. Soon the people will begin to doubt my powers. Then they'll be questioning my authority."

Two Heads stepped back, indignant and startled, and looked intently into the face of the high priest.

"If they dare to question your authority," he said, "we should kill them."

Standing-in-the-Doorway smiled, a weak, sad and indulgent smile. He ran a hand through the young man's hair.

"We can't kill them all," he said. "No. I must bring the rain. And soon."

"What will you do?" asked Two Heads.

"Thunder lives in the west," Standing-in-the-Doorway said. "Far to the west. Once, in my youth, a young man went to search for him and was never seen again. Now someone else will have to try. Thunder will have to be found. I'm going to have to send someone west to look for Thunder and to bring back the rain."

"Who will you send?" said Two Heads. "Me? Will I have to go?"

Standing-in-the-Doorway chuckled softly and reached out again for Two Heads. He pulled him close and held him.

"No," he said. "Not you. I would miss you too much. But three priests will go. I'll choose them soon."

Edohi had left the deer at his mother's house, and he was walking toward the *gatayusti* playing field. Something might be happening there. If nothing else, he thought, he would almost certainly find some men sitting around talking. But he didn't make it to the *gatayusti* field. Corn Flower stepped out from behind a house and stopped him.

" *'Siyo,* Edohi," she said. "I haven't seen you for a while."

" *'Siyo,* Corn Flower," he said. "I've been away a great deal."

"Yes, I know," she said. "Where were you today? Were you hunting?"

"Yes."

"And were you successful in your hunt?"

"I brought my mother a deer," he said. "A big one."

"I guessed as much," said Corn Flower. "You always bring back something."

"No," he said. "Not always."

"That's what everyone says about you. Edohi never comes back empty-handed. That's what they say."

Edohi shrugged and shuffled his feet. He was looking at the ground. It was an awkward moment. He was trying to find a graceful way to excuse himself and get away from her, but he couldn't think of what to say.

"You've been avoiding me," she said, suddenly surprisingly blunt. "I don't know why. We used to be such good friends. Don't you like me anymore?"

"Of course I like you," said Edohi. "It's just that things are different now. We're not children anymore. It used to be the three of us. Always. Me and you and Acorn."

"You mean Two Heads, the priest?" she said, her voice betraying a cynical displeasure.

"I mean Acorn," said Edohi. "Anyway, he's gone. We're grown. Things are not the way they used to be."

"Because Acorn is gone, you don't want to see me anymore?"

"No. That's not what I mean. I feel differently about you now. It started just before that time the Choctaws captured us. I didn't understand it, though."

"Do you understand it now?"

"When we were young," said Edohi, "you were just another friend. But I began to see you—as a woman."

Corn Flower blushed slightly. "Do you like what you see?" she asked.

"You're beautiful," said Edohi. "There's never been anyone like you."

"Then why have you stayed away from me?" she said.

"When we changed, when we grew up and my feelings for you changed, I didn't know what your feelings would be. I didn't know what you would think of me—in that way. We were just—playmates."

"Edohi," said Corn Flower, "my feelings for you are different, too. But I still want to be with you. I've missed you."

"And I missed you," he said.

Edohi did not sleep well that night. His mind was too active, and his thoughts were all of Corn Flower. She had practically told him that she would marry him, that she wanted him to live with her and be her man. He had spent so much time worrying about his feelings for her, only to find out that she, too, had such feelings. He was ecstatic over that news, but it had brought him a new dilemma.

Ayasta. The Spoiler. Edohi realized that he was actually afraid of Corn Flower's mother. What would the Spoiler think of him, a young man with no honors, no experience of war? Why, the Spoiler had earned her own war honors. Would she not insist that any man asking for her daughter have as much? He would have to do something, he knew, to earn the respect of the Spoiler. Only then would he be able to ask for her daughter.

Eleven

WAR WOMAN was sitting beneath an arbor which stood beside her house when she saw the contingent approaching. Standing-in-the-Doorway had chosen to walk rather than be carried in his litter chair, but he was accompanied by four lesser priests. They were not yet close enough to the arbor to eavesdrop on normal conversation when he stopped them and spoke to them. Then he walked on alone to the arbor, the others waiting patiently and respectfully where he left them.

" *'Siyo*, brother," said War Woman. "What brings you to my house?"

" *'Siyo*," he said. He sat on a low bench in the shade of the arbor. The heat was still oppressive. "I've come to confer with you on a matter of great importance."

"The rain," she said.

"Yes."

"It's bad. Even the river is low. If it doesn't rain soon, we will have real trouble here."

"Have you heard any reports of grumblings from the people?"

"No more than what I have just said," said War Woman.

"No one questioning my power and authority?"

"No."

"They will if I don't bring rain soon."

War Woman slowly nodded her head. "But they won't say anything around me," she said.

"I'm going to send three priests to the west," said Standing-in-the-Doorway, "to search for Thunder and to bring back the rain."

War Woman looked her brother in the eyes, but only for an instant. She looked away again.

"That has never been done," she said. "Not in my lifetime."

"What else would you suggest?" said Standing-in-the-Doorway. He stood and paced the length of the arbor. "I've done everything else. I'm— It's a desperate situation."

"Yes, it is," she agreed. "I suppose there's nothing else to do. Yes. You should send them. The people need to know that you are doing everything possible. Who will you send?"

"That's why I've come to you. I'm thinking of Kanegwati, Water Moccasin, to be in charge. He's old enough to have some wisdom, yet young enough to make the journey."

"And he's been a warrior. I agree. Who else?"

"Etawa Tsistatlaski," said Standing-in-the-Doorway. "Deadwood Lighter. He's ambitious. And this is a very dangerous mission. If things go wrong, Deadwood Lighter will not be missed too much."

War Woman nodded her head. "You said three," she said.

"I've not chosen the third. Who do you think should go?"

War Woman wrinkled her brow in thought. She stood and stared off toward the west.

"It must be a long way west to Thunder's house," she said. "As far as I can see in that direction, there are no clouds. There would have to be clouds near Thunder's house, don't you think?"

"Who do you think should go?" said Standing-in-the-Doorway.

"This will be an important journey," said War Woman. "It will be a thing that people will talk about for years to come. The third man should be a scribe. He'll need to keep a record of the trip."

"We have but few scribes," said Standing-in-the-Doorway. "It would be a loss if one did not return."

"You asked for my opinion," said War Woman. "I've given it to you."

"Yes," said the priest. He stepped out from under the arbor, folded his arms across his chest and turned to face his sister again. "Of course, you're right. Iya-Iyusdi is the youngest of the scribes, and he's not much good for anything else. It's settled then. Like-a-Pumpkin will be the third."

Edohi walked down by the river. Children were splashing in the water, seeking relief from the intense heat, so he walked farther downstream until he was alone, and he sat there at the water's edge. He noticed again how low the water had gotten. He stared at the water as it flowed past him, and he wondered where it all was going. He listened to its voice, but he couldn't understand any words. For a while he sat in silence. All his life, Edohi had gone to Hemp Carrier for advice. Now he could not. Hemp Carrier would not be able to help, for this was a thing that Edohi would have to do for himself. How could he make himself worthy of the daughter of the Spoiler? He strained to hear a message in the voice of the river, Long Man, and the waters babbled to his ears: Ayasta, Ayasta, Ayasta.

He stood up and went back into the village to find Hemp Carrier. His uncle was lounging in front of the townhouse, talking and smoking with friends. Edohi nodded a greeting to his uncle and the other men and stood by politely waiting. Hemp Carrier could tell that Edohi had a need to talk with him privately, but it would not be polite for him to walk away from a discussion. Kick Up was talking, and Edohi squatted at the edge of the group and pretended to listen.

"My mother's garden is pitiful," Kick Up was saying, "We've all been busy carrying water to the town's garden. Then we're too tired to carry more water to my mother's garden, so it suffers."

Edohi thought that Kick Up must be lazy, for he knew that his own mother was working in the town's garden and in her own, and he and his father had both been worn out carrying water for her to both gardens. It was true that they needed rain, but there was always the river. Of course, he kept these thoughts to himself.

"We need rain," said Agili.

"And why don't we have rain?" said Hemp Carrier. "Why? It's unnatural for things to get so dry. Something's wrong somewhere. And who is responsible? It's not you and me. We're not responsible for the rain."

"Be careful what you say," said Kick Up.

"Do you mean that I shouldn't say that the *Ani-Kutani*

are responsible for the lack of rain? I shouldn't mention the fact that they have charge of all public ceremonies? I guess I shouldn't even suggest that perhaps their usurpation of powers which were never rightly theirs might have thrown us all out of balance. I won't say those things then. I won't say that the priests are to blame."

The others were all silent. They looked at the ground or looked away. After a moment of this uneasy silence, Hemp Carrier looked at Edohi.

"Ah," he said, "what do I know?"

He walked over to stand beside Edohi, and Edohi stood up. Hemp Carrier put a hand on his shoulder to guide him away from the group, and he walked with his nephew over to the edge of the *gatayusti* field. No one else was near.

"So, nephew," he said, "what is it?"

"What?" said Edohi.

"Did you want me for some reason?"

Edohi looked at the ground and shuffled his feet. "Can you tell me about the Spoiler?" he said.

"The Spoiler? What do you want to know about the Spoiler?"

"She has war honors," said Edohi. "Not many women have war honors."

"That's true."

"How did she get them? Do you know?"

"It was a long time ago," said Hemp Carrier, "when you were just starting to walk, and I was a young man. The Real People were at war with *Ani-Sawahani.* We're still at war with them, I guess. The war was never ended, even though it's been some years now since they have raided us or we have raided them.

"Anyway, the Spoiler was a young woman then. Her husband was Tunai, and Corn Flower, like you, was just beginning to walk. With some other people from Ijodi, they had been visiting at one of our far northern towns, Chilhowee, maybe: maybe it was farther north. I don't remember. But they were coming home, and it was a long way. They had stopped along the road to camp, and a party of *Ani-Sawahani* was suddenly upon them. Tunai was killed almost before anyone could react. The Shawnees outnumbered our people, but only by one or two, I think. The Real People rallied quickly and fought back. Some Shawnees were killed, and another of our own people was killed, too. Then the Shawnees ran. The Real People were beating them, but one grabbed the little Corn Flower up in his arms before he ran. The Spoiler, who was kneeling beside her slain husband, took the warclub from his body and ran after the Shawnee who was stealing her daughter. She could run fast in those days. She caught him and split his skull.

"Some of the others from the camp had followed her, men and women, and the Spoiler left her daughter with the women and went with the men to catch the rest of the Shawnees. They caught them and killed them all. All but one. They let one live to get back home and tell the tale. The Spoiler killed two of them, two more, with her dead husband's warclub."

Edohi was silent for a moment. He tried to imagine Corn Flower's mother wielding a warclub, fighting men, but he could not. It was an amazing story, and, of course, he believed it, even though it astonished him.

"So she had her revenge," he said.

"She never thought so," said Hemp Carrier. "I've heard her say that one hundred Shawnees would not be enough to pay for the loss of her Tunai. And even lately I've heard her say how she longs to have a Shawnee slave.

No. Time has not yet healed her wound. You know she never remarried."

Iya-Iyusdi, Like-a-Pumpkin, was a little frightened at the prospect of the long journey which he had been assigned to make. He had never before been outside the territory of the Real People. He was a little frightened, yet he was excited at the thought of going on such an important mission. He had never before felt important, really important, except when he had been chosen to learn the writing. He had felt important then, because the writing was both secret and sacred. Not even all of the priests were allowed to know the writing. Yet there were others who knew it, and gradually he had come to believe that the only reason he had been selected to become a scribe was that he couldn't seem to do anything else very well. Even when he had scored the winning point in the ball game against the Choctaws, that had been almost an accident. He had just been standing there, and the ball had come to him. He had run between the goals like a scared rabbit. But going to search for Thunder, to bring back the rain, that was important.

In his tiny house inside the walls of Men's Town, he prepared for the journey, and he recalled the old tale of the boy who had gone to look for Thunder.

The boy lived alone with his mother in a house outside the village. Even though they lived away from other people, the boy seldom went outside the house. He was ashamed to be seen, for his body was covered all over with ugly sores. His mother had tried everything she could think of, and so had all the doctors from around where they lived. Nothing helped. Eventually the boy's mother took pity on him, so miserable was he.

"There is a way you might be cured," she said.

"What is it?" said the boy, leaping to his feet. "Tell me. I'll try anything."

"First I must tell you an old secret," she said. "Before you were born, Thunder came to visit me. I was young and unmarried, and Thunder was in the form of a beautiful young man. We made love together, and that's when you were conceived. Thunder is your father."

The boy could hardly believe the story his mother was telling him. He stared at her with his eyes wide and his mouth hanging open.

"Thunder is the greatest of all doctors," she said. "If you go find your father, he'll cure you of those spots."

So she made him some new clothes and prepared some food for him to take and sent him on his way.

"Where does my father live?" he asked her.

"To the west," she said.

The boy began his journey, walking west. Every time he came to a village, or to a lone house, or met someone along the way, he stopped to ask the people if they knew where Thunder lived.

"To the west," they always answered.

He had traveled for a long time, and he was weary. The new clothes his mother had made for him looked old and ragged. Then he came to a house which stood alone. In front of the house was a cleared, circular playing field, and there was a man standing at the edge of the field, playing a game with a stone wheel and a spear. The man was Untsaiyi, also called the Gambler, and the game he played was the *gatayusti* game. The Gambler saw the boy and called out to him, asking him to play. It was a gambling game, and he wanted to bet.

"I haven't time," the boy said.

"Take time for just one game."

"I have nothing to bet."

"I'll play for your pretty spots," the Gambler said.

The boy was hurt and embarrassed at the Gambler's cruelly comic reference to his sores, but he tried not to let it show.

"I have to find the house of Thunder," he said. "Can you tell me where he lives?"

"Of course I can," said the Gambler. "If you play a game with me, I'll tell you."

"If you tell me where he lives, I'll stop and play on my way back."

"Oh, all right," said the Gambler. "He's very near. I hear him all the time, rumbling away over there. His house is just beyond the next hill. That one right there. But don't forget your promise to come back and play."

The boy assured the Gambler that he'd return and play a game, and then he hurried on to find the house of Thunder. But when he got there, Thunder was waiting for him. He already knew that the boy was coming, and he knew what the boy wanted. He also knew that the boy claimed to be his son. But Thunder had known many women, and any boy, he thought, would be proud to be his son. This boy might easily be an impostor. He would have to be tested. He met the boy in front of his house.

"What do you want with me?" he demanded.

"My mother told me that you're my father," said the boy. "She also told me that you're a great doctor. I've come to ask you to cure me of these sores."

Thunder looked the boy over.

"Hmm," he said. "Come in."

Inside he pointed toward a chair fashioned of thorny vines. The long sharp thorns stuck out all over.

"Sit down," he said.

The boy sat in the chair and appeared to be content.

This boy might be my son, thought Thunder. I'll cure him of his sores, but then I'll test him further. He called his wife and had her put a pot of water on the fire to boil, and while it boiled, he threw in various herbs. Then he picked the boy up and threw him in. The boy stayed in the boiling water. He didn't scream, and he didn't flinch. He even smiled.

"Take him down to the river and throw him in," Thunder said to his wife.

She picked up the pot of boiling water with the boy still in it and walked to the water's edge. When she threw it in, there was a great splash and a hissing and a cloud of steam. Where the pot went in an eddy was formed, and when the steam cleared, the boy was there clinging to the roots of a service tree that grew there on the bank. The spots were no longer on the boy. They were on the tree.

Thunder's wife pulled the boy out of the water, and she saw that he was handsome.

"I know that you are Thunder's son," she said, "but Thunder is suspicious. He'll have some more tests for you. On our way back to the house, I'll tell you what they are and what to do."

When Thunder's wife took the boy back into the house, Thunder looked at the boy.

"So," he said, "your spots are gone."

"Yes," said the boy. "*Wado.* Thank you."

"But now I think you need new clothes."

Thunder's wife gave the boy some beautiful new buckskin leggings, a breechclout and new moccasins. Then Thunder pointed to a large basket with a lid.

"Get yourself some new jewelry from there," he said.

The boy had been prepared by Thunder's wife for what was about to happen. He lifted the lid and saw that the basket was filled with writhing snakes, but without hesitation, he plunged his arm into the squirming mass all the way to the bottom. He grasped a snake down there and pulled it out. It was *ujonati*, a rattlesnake, and he wrapped it around his neck for a necklace. Then he reached in again and pulled out a copperhead, which he wound around one wrist for a bracelet. He reached in a third time and brought out another copperhead. That made the bracelet for his other wrist.

Thunder was almost convinced by this that the boy was indeed his son, but there was yet one final test. He called his two sons who lived with him, Anisgaya-tsunsdiga, the Little Men or Little Thunders, sometimes called the Thunder Boys, and he took all three boys outside and gave them ballsticks and a ball and had them play, the boy who claimed to be his son against the other two. As the Thunder Boys ran and struck the ball, their thunderclaps resounded, but as the other boy darted back and forth on the playing field, lightning flashed, for he was the son of Thunder, and he was Lightning.

When Anagalisgi, or Lightning, grew tired of the ball play, acting on instructions Thunder's wife had given him, he struck a honey locust tree which stood beside the field, and Thunder stopped the game. It was his favorite tree, and he was afraid that Lightning would destroy it.

"I know that you're my son," he said.

"Father," said Lightning, "on my way to find you, I stopped to ask directions at a house not far from here. A man there asked me to play a game with him and to bet, but I would not. He had a stone wheel and a spear."

"Ah," said Thunder, "that was my neighbor, the Gambler. It's good you didn't play with him. He cheats. He hates to lose, and when he loses, he bets more and more until he has nothing left to bet except his life. Then when he loses that, he runs away."

"But I promised him that I would stop back by and play," said Lightning.

"Then we will see that you win and you collect," said Thunder, and he gave instructions to Lightning and sent him on his way with a long-necked gourd.

"So you've come back," said the Gambler, "and without your spots. What do you have to bet?"

A string of beads dangled from a hole in the end of the long-necked gourd, and Lightning started to pull on the beads. The strand kept coming. It circled the playing field four times, and still it had no end.

"This many beads," said Lightning.

They played the game, and Lightning won, and then they played again. They played until the Gambler had nothing left to bet.

"Let's play again," he said. "If you win this time, you can have my wife."

They played again, and Lightning won again.

"You have nothing left to bet," said Lightning.

"Play one more game," said the Gambler. "If I lose this time, my life is yours. You can kill me."

The Gambler lost again, and then he really had nothing left to bet.

"Let me go into my house and tell my wife what's happened here," he said. "Then you can kill me and take her."

Lightning agreed, and the Gambler went inside, but the Gambler's unusual house had two doors, and he escaped out the back and ran. Lightning called for his brothers, and they appeared, and they started to chase the Gambler. They finally caught him at the far western edge of the land. They tied his arms with a grapevine, and they ran a long pole through his middle and pinned him down to the ocean floor. He'll be there until the end of the world, for the Gambler cannot die.

Like-a-Pumpkin thought about the story and wondered just how long the trip would be. The story didn't say. He wondered if he would find the house of Thunder, if he'd see Thunder and his wife and sons. He wondered if the Gambler still was on the ocean floor, or if he'd managed to escape. He wondered if he'd see the Gambler. Most of all he wondered if he and his companions would be able to bring back the rain. He hoped that they would, and he prayed for their success. He prayed to Asgaya Gigagei, Red Man, the Thunderer himself. Then he began meticulously to gather up his brushes, his "book" of pounded, folded bark and the black walnut pigment he used to make his ink.

Edohi equipped himself with a wooden, ball-headed warclub, a sharp flint knife, a strong ash bow with half a dozen river cane, flint-tipped arrows and a length of twisted rawhide rope. He said goodbye to his mother, but he did not tell her where he was going. He left Ijodi in the morning, just as the sun was peeking out from under the eastern edge of the Sky Vault. He headed north and a little west. He headed for the land of *Ani-Sawahani*, the land of the Shawnee People. He had a plan.

Water Moccasin, Deadwood Lighter and Like-a-Pumpkin left Men's Town walking due west. Each carried a small bundle and a staff. They wore knee-length tunics made of a rough tan cloth woven from plant fibers which marked them as priests. On the central mound, in front of the temple in Men's Town, Standing-in-the-Doorway stood and watched them go. According to all of the stories of the Real People, the task he had assigned them made perfect sense. Thunder lived in the west, and Thunder was a friend to the Real People. In the past, others had gone west and found Thunder, had spoken to him. The three priests should be able to travel west and find their goal. Yet there would be dangers, and Standing-in-the-Doorway had no idea how long he would have to wait for the return of his priests, how far away the house of Thunder might be, how long the journey should take. He wasn't even really sure there really would be an actual house out there with a being who looked like a man, who could talk with them, who lived there, who would be Thunder. Secretly, Standing-in-the-Doorway thought that the stories were only stories, that they were told to the people to teach them lessons and to give them explanations for things that otherwise they would not be able to understand. And secretly he thought, as he watched the three priests slowly disappear down the road, that he would never see them again, that he had sent them to their deaths. But he had had no choice. They needed rain, and the people expected Standing-in-the-Doorway to do something. So he had sent the priests.

Twelve

THEY HAD BEEN WALKING for four days, and Like-a-Pumpkin knew that they still had far to go. Yet never before had he walked four days west from his home. It was a long way. The country was unfamiliar. Oh, there was nothing he could not identify. There were oaks and elms and ash, hickory and locust trees. Yet it was somehow different. He did not know the road, even though it was the same road he had started out on from Men's Town. It seemed strange to him that the same road he walked so far from home went right back to his town. All that way. The same road. But the other end. The western end. That was the question. What would they find at the western end of the road? He did not know of anyone who had walked to the western end of the road, who had found the home of Thunder and returned to the land of the Real People to tell about it.

Of course, there were stories, stories from the long-ago times, the times when the earth was yet young. Like-a-Pumpkin felt a pang of guilt as he found himself wondering if the stories were true. Did Thunder really live in the west? And did the young boy really travel from the land of the Real People to Thunder's home and become Lightning? He had heard the old stories, had learned them, had even repeated them without ever questioning their veracity, but walking the road to the west, going on a journey to seek out the house of Thunder, his mind began to question them. Deadwood Lighter interrupted Like-a-Pumpkin's thoughts with a question.

"How close to the edge of the world, do you think, is Thunder's house?" he said.

"Oh," said Like-a-Pumpkin, "I don't know."

"Do we know," asked Water Moccasin, "if Thunder lives on this side of the Sky Vault? Or on the other?"

"In the story about Lightning," said Like-a-Pumpkin, "there is no mention of the boy going under the Vault."

"Maybe it was left out," said Water Moccasin. "There is no mention of the boy stopping along his way to relieve himself either, but he must have done so. A story cannot include every detail."

"That's true," said Deadwood Lighter. "And in the story of Kanati, the Great Hunter, and Selu, his wife and our Corn Mother, whom we also believe to be Thunder and his wife, at the end, they live on top of the Sky Vault."

Maybe, thought Like-a-Pumpkin, the stories are not true, for they do not always fit together the way it seems that they should. He found himself almost hoping that they were not true, for if they turned out to be true, the things awaiting them at the end of the westward journey were frightening. His mind recalled the story of the men who went to find the sun.

The earth is flat, like a plate, and it's floating on water. The Sky Vault is like a great bowl sitting upside down over the plate. It is made of solid rock. When it is daylight on this earth, the sun is on the underside of the Vault. At night, she is on the topside. Six men wondered about her. They decided to go find out where she lives and how she gets from the topside of the Vault to the underside. They traveled west for a long time. They wore out all of their extra moccasins and ate up all the dried corn they had taken with them. Along the way they met many different kinds of people with languages they had never heard before. They met people who did not even know the trade jargon with which people of different tongues at home could talk to one another. Some of the people they met tried to talk to them with hand signs. Sometimes they could make out the meaning of the signs. Sometimes they could not.

When at last they arrived at the western edge, the sun was very near. It was close to the end of a day. They looked at her, and they saw that she had the form of a woman, but they had to look away again quickly because she was so bright. Then, as the sun came close to the ground, an amazing thing happened. The great Sky Vault began to tilt, and a space opened up between the Vault and the earth. The sun crawled under the Vault, headed for the other side.

One of the men ran after her, but the other five were afraid, and they stayed back. When the man was under the thick edge of the Vault, and there was yet a glimmer of light from the sun, who had disappeared, the Vault started back down. They heard their companion scream, and they saw the beginning of his end as the Vault descended right on top of him. But they didn't see it all. As the mighty Vault crushed him to death, they were engulfed in darkness. They spent a restless night waiting for the sun to reemerge in the east. When she did, they started home, and by the time they got back to the land of the Real People, they were old men. But they told the tale, and that was the way the Real People learned that the sun crawls along the underside of the Sky Vault, goes out under on the western edge, then crawls along the topside to the eastern edge to crawl back under and start the journey all over again. Her journey takes a day and a night.

If the story is true, thought Like-a-Pumpkin, and if Thunder's house is on the other side, then we will have to go under. Will we be crushed to death the same as the man in the story? If we live through this adventure, will we return home old men? And if it takes that long for us to bring back the rain, will our whole country be dried up and dead by then? Is all of our effort to be in vain?

"I guess we'll find out when we get there," he said.

Deadwood Lighter, who was walking between the other two men, put out his arms to stop them.

"If we get there at all," he said. "Look up ahead."

Six men, dressed and armed as if for war, came out of the woods to block the road.

"*Ani-Tsiksu?*" asked Water Moccasin.

"I think so," said Deadwood Lighter. "They look like Chickasaw People to me, and I think that we're in the Chickasaw country still."

"What shall we do?" asked Like-a-Pumpkin. "Run?"

"They have long bows," said Water Moccasin. "If we turn and run, they could easily shoot us in our backs from that distance."

"We can't fight them," said Like-a-Pumpkin. "There are six of them and only three of us, and they are well armed."

"We'll talk to them," said Deadwood Lighter. "Come on."

They walked on toward the waiting Chickasaws, and Like-a-Pumpkin felt his heart begin to pound more rapidly and harder inside his chest. There were plenty of dangers along the way, he realized. He didn't need to be worrying yet about what waited at the end of the road. When they got close enough for conversation, one of the Chickasaws spoke first.

"You are *Chalakee* priests," he said, using the trade jargon.

"Yes," said Deadwood Lighter.

"What are priests doing so far away from home?"

"We're going on a journey to find the house of Thunder in the west. Our task is to bring back the rain."

The Chickasaw turned to his companions, and they had a hurried conversation in their own language. Like-a-Pumpkin hoped that they could not hear his heart pounding, could not see his knees shake. Then the Chickasaw spoke again in the jargon.

"We thought to kill you," he said. "Some *Chalakees* killed some of our people not long ago. But we all need rain. The earth is drying up. Our crops are puny. Since you're going for the rain, we'll let you go in peace and hope that you succeed, but when we see you coming back, if it hasn't rained by then, we'll kill you."

The priests walked on, and when Like-a-Pumpkin at last felt bold enough to look back over his shoulder, he saw no sign of the six Chickasaw warriors. He thought, we'll have to be more careful from here on. The next time, we might not be so lucky.

Edohi was in the land of the Shawnees. He was almost certain of that. For two days he had seen no one, but he felt sure that he would find a village soon. He had begun to exercise even more than usual caution. He no longer used the trail. The chances of avoiding contact with someone were better in the woods. Yet he stayed near the trail, for the trail would lead to a village. It had to lead somewhere. The first three days, he had hunted for his food, but deep in the country of his enemies, he ate mostly his parched corn. If he killed some game, he would have to build a fire to cook it, and smoke from the fire could give away his presence to the Shawnees. He noticed that the trail he followed had begun to run alongside a meandering stream, and he thought that might be an indication that a town was not far ahead. The stream and trail were to his right. Ahead and to his left the mountains rose. He would climb the mountain so he could look down on the trail and on the village which he felt sure that he would find.

He had not been back to Ijodi since he had become Two Heads, and he had asked Standing-in-the-Doorway for permission to make a visit. To see his mother, he had said. In reality, Two Heads did not want to visit his mother. He was a little surprised at himself that he had not missed her. In fact, he had noticed recently that his former life as Acorn seemed almost like a dream. It seemed like someone else's life that he had simply watched and known about. Now he understood, he thought, the real significance of a name change, for now he was Two Heads. He was not Acorn.

Yet he wanted to visit Ijodi. He wanted the people who lived there, the people who had known Acorn, to see him as Two Heads the priest, the *kutani*. Acorn had been insignificant. Two Heads was important. He wanted them all to see him. He wanted Sparrow to see. He wanted most of all for Corn Flower to see. He hated Corn Flower. He hated her for always besting him at everything they did.

He hated her for the squirrel she had killed and given him. He hated her because she'd saved him from the Choctaws. Most of all he hated her for the way she had stood before the entire population of Ijodi and bragged of what she had done, while he sat by alone, ignored and scorned. She had been treated like a triumphant warrior. He hated her, and he had to see her.

He stopped at his mother's house and ate, and he noticed that he no longer had a taste for the food that she prepared. He was formal, polite but aloof, and he excused himself soon after he had finished his meal. He had no reason to stay. There was nothing for him to talk to this woman about, and he found her questions about his new life tedious and slightly irritating. He left, and he walked around the streets of Ijodi, his arms crossed over his chest, his head held high. When people greeted him, he spoke to some, simply gave others a haughty nod. He had to show them that he knew his place, and that his place was much higher than theirs.

"He's even more arrogant than Standing-in-the-Doorway," someone whispered to a companion as he walked on by. He knew that they were talking about him behind his back, but he didn't care. Whatever they were saying, they didn't dare say it to his face, and that knowledge was to Two Heads a deep, warm joy. Then he saw her. She was walking toward him. He could see that she recognized him and that she was surprised. He stopped and stood, waiting for her to approach.

" 'Siyo," she said, and she hesitated before speaking his new name, "Two Heads."

" 'Siyo, Corn Flower, playmate of my childhood."

"You've changed," she said. "Are you happy in your new life?"

"I am someone of importance now," he said.

"Yes," she said. "I'm happy for you."

"I haven't seen our old companion here today," said Two Heads. "Our Sparrow."

"He's Edohi now," said Corn Flower. "He's away. He's usually away. That's how he got his new name."

"Of course. I knew all that," said Two Heads. "The great hunter. They talk like he's Kanati himself. It's just as well that he's gone today. I no longer have any reason to see him. I'm not a child anymore. I have an important position now. I wouldn't even bother to come here, but I thought I should visit my mother. It makes her proud to see me in my robes."

Corn Flower suddenly wished that Two Heads would go away. He had always been sullen and pouty and self-indulgent, but now he had become an arrogant, self-centered man. He obviously felt he was better than his old friends, that he was above the people of Ijodi, even somehow above his own mother. Corn Flower had never had much patience with Acorn, but even she had been unprepared for the disgusting man he would become. Was it the priesthood that had made him thus, or would he have grown to this no matter what? She wondered.

"Walk with me," said Two Heads. It was not a request. It was a demand. Corn Flower didn't like it, but she walked. He led her to the river's edge, and then he walked away from town, beyond the prying eyes of others. He strolled, casually, as if he had no destination in mind, no purpose at hand, and he made small talk as he strolled. Then, abruptly, he stopped and turned to face her. His eyes narrowed to slits, and a slight smirk spread across his lips. He hated her, but he wanted her. He had to show her that he was a man, and he had to show himself. He reached out toward her with his right hand, and she recoiled.

Thirteen

THE SPOILER dipped a large bottle gourd into the river and allowed it to fill about halfway. Had she completely filled the gourd, it would have been too heavy to carry. As she stood up, she saw her daughter approaching. Corn Flower had a haughty look about her, something about her carriage, the way she stepped, the way she held her head.

"Corn Flower?" said the Spoiler.

" '*Siyo*, Mother," said Corn Flower. "Let me carry that for you."

Corn Flower took the heavy gourd and headed up toward the village.

"To your garden?" she asked.

"Yes," said the Spoiler. She wanted to ask Corn Flower if something was wrong, but if Corn Flower had something she wanted her mother to know, she'd tell her. The Spoiler stood for a moment beside the river watching her daughter walk away. Then she saw Two Heads. He was coming from the same direction as had Corn Flower. His look was sullen, and his robe was wet. He turned away from the river as soon as he could. He seemed to be trying to avoid contact with anyone.

Other people, men and children as well as women, were starting to come to the river with bottle gourds or pottery vessels to carry water. They had been so long without rain that the gardens would all dry up if they failed to carry water to them regularly. It was hard work, backbreaking work, but it had to be done. The Spoiler watched the gardeners coming to the river, and she watched Two Heads sulk away, and she wondered what had happened down there. Then a woman spoke to her.

"Are you here to watch the rest of us work?"

"Ha," said the Spoiler, and she turned and followed the path of her daughter. For a long time that day they carried water. Back and forth they went. And Corn Flower did not tell her mother anything about her encounter with Two Heads.

The village was not quite like any they had ever seen before. To begin with, the landscape had finally undergone a significant change. There were still hills and trees, but there were also vast prairies, nearly flat expanses where few or no trees grew. They found the village close to the big river. They had never seen a river so wide, and they were trying to figure out how they would cross it when the people had appeared, a small group, a family, Like-a-Pumpkin guessed. There were two men, two women and three small children, all nearly naked. The men wore their hair cropped just at shoulder length. The women wore theirs in two long braids. They wore no jewelry. Deadwood Lighter spoke to the people, and the oldest man among them replied, but their language was strange to the ears of the priests of the Real People. They could not understand each other. Deadwood Lighter tried the trade jargon, but the naked people only looked at one another and shrugged.

Then Like-a-Pumpkin made signs at them, trying to signify that they were going west and that they wanted to cross the river. The old man looked puzzled for a moment, then smiled. He gestured to the priests to follow as he spoke in his strange language to his family. Then he led them all to the village. It was surrounded by a palisade fence, much like those used by the Real People, but the logs were bare, not plastered. It looked to Like-a-Pumpkin like an unfinished wall. And there were corn fields outside the fence. But inside were houses covered with bark. There was no townhouse, no central plaza. The other people inside were, like the family they had met at the river's edge, practically naked.

"They seem to be very poor people," said Water Moccasin.

Yet these poor people prepared a feast for their unannounced guests, and everyone ate very well. There were several kinds of meat and fish and several varieties of corn and beans. It was by far the best meal the three *Ani-Kutani* had eaten since having left Men's Town. They smiled much, nodded their heads wildly and pointed at the food in attempts to convey thanks and compliments. Their host smiled and nodded in response. When the sun was low on the western edge of the Sky Vault, the host people showed the priests to a house. The bark covering, the rounded roof and the smaller size gave the house a different appearance from those used by the Real People, but once he was inside, Like-a-Pumpkin decided that they were not really so different after all.

There were only two cots in the house, and Like-a-Pumpkin volunteered to sleep on the ground. Deadwood

Lighter and Water Moccasin went to bed, but Like-a-Pumpkin went back outside. A small fire burned just in front of the house, and Like-a-Pumpkin spread out his bark pages there on the ground in the meager light of the flames. He mixed some water with some of his pigment, dipped in a brush and started to write. Each character he painted stood for a syllable in the language of the Real People. There were over eighty characters, and Like-a-Pumpkin had mastered them rather quickly. He had also been praised among the scribes of the *Ani-Kutani* for the beauty of the characters as he painted them. He wrote:

We have stopped this night at a village of strange people. Their language is unintelligible to us as ours to them. Nor do they seem to know the trade language that we use. They wear no clothes and no jewelry and seem to be exceedingly poor, except they do not seem to want for food. They have treated us well and fed us well. We tried to converse with them by means of signs, and we think that we have made them know that we need to cross the wide river which runs here by their town, and that our mission is to go west to bring back the rain. I think that they will help us cross the river in the morning. The country here is hot and dry just as we left it at home. These people, I think, have been carrying river water in jugs to water their gardens. It will be to everyone's benefit when we bring back the rain.

Like-a-Pumpkin looked up from his work and stared off toward the west. His mind repeated the last few words he had written. When we bring back the rain. It occurred to him that he might have been more accurate and honest had he written "if we bring back the rain." The night was clear, bright with stars. There were no clouds to obscure their light.

Two Heads sat sullen and morose in the darkness of the room in the temple at Men's Town. Standing-in-the-Doorway watched him in silence for a moment. Then he spoke.

"The visit to your mother seems to have upset you," he said.

"I'm all right," said Two Heads.

"Tell me about your day in Ijodi. Tell me everything."

Two Heads looked at Standing-in-the-Doorway, then looked away again. There was something about the man that Two Heads could not define, something great and powerful, frightening, yet a little sad. He knew that he could not lie to Standing-in-the-Doorway, could not even fail to tell the whole truth. Something in his mind suggested to him that perhaps Standing-in-the-Doorway already knew everything anyway. The man was like a god.

"I did go to see my mother," said Two Heads, "but I didn't stay. I walked around the town. I wanted the people to see me."

"Go on," said Standing-in-the-Doorway.

"I found Corn Flower, one of my old playmates, the one who gave you the squirrels when first we met."

"Yes, I remember," said Standing-in-the-Doorway.

"We talked awhile, and I asked her to walk with me down by the river."

"Away from the eyes and ears of others?"

Two Heads ducked his head in shame. He felt his face grow hot, and he was glad that he sat in darkness.

"So you wanted a woman?" said Standing-in-the-Doorway.

"Yes."

"That particular woman?"

"Yes."

"It's all right. I'm not angry with you. So long as you come back here to me, it's all right. Did this woman satisfy your lust?"

Two Heads sat in silence for a moment. He began to tremble.

"She threw me in the river," he blurted out at once, and he began to sob convulsively. Standing-in-the-Doorway moved to his side and put an arm around his shoulders. He held the young man tight against him for a moment.

"Calm yourself," he said. "There are other women, and there are better things than women."

"She made a fool of me," said Two Heads. "She always has. I hate her."

"I see."

Standing-in-the-Doorway stood up and walked to the door. He looked out into the clear sky.

"Perhaps one day before long," he said, "you'll have a chance to get your revenge. This land is drier every day. More streams dry up. The river gets lower. If those three who have gone west fail to bring back the rain, there will be sterner measures called for soon."

In the morning the naked people carried dugout canoes to the water's edge and, with signs, made it known to the three traveling priests that they would take them across the river. Like-a-Pumpkin was afraid. It was the widest river he had ever seen, and its current was swift. The dugouts, which were much like those used by his own people, seemed awfully small, inadequate for the task. Yet they had to cross the water, and he could think of no other way. Three boats were launched. Each carried two oarsmen and one priest. Like-a-Pumpkin wondered if that was a strategy intended to get at least one of them safely across. If one boat capsized, then two priests would survive. If two boats were lost, one priest would live to pursue their mission. But what if the great river chose to swallow all three boats? That prospect seemed to Like-a-Pumpkin to be a likely one, at least as likely as any other.

Sitting in the middle of the dugout, Like-a-Pumpkin silently made a prayer to Long Man, but he worried that this Long Man would not understand his speech. Perhaps it would only understand the speech of his strange-talking, naked hosts. Had they spoken to the river? He couldn't tell. He could only hope that they had. He listened to the sounds of the river and strained to perceive meaning, any kind of meaning, a word of comfort, a warning. But the voice of the river was like the voice of the naked people, and it carried no sense to the ears of Like-a-Pumpkin. He gripped the sides of the boat tightly as the two oarsmen waded into the waters pushing and pulling the heavy boat along with them.

A river this wide must be very deep, Like-a-Pumpkin thought, and his mind began to imagine the mysteries lurking in its depths. He wondered if the frightful *ukitena* kind had wandered this far west. He had never seen an *uk'ten'*, but he knew all of the tales. And some conjurers among the Real People even possessed their powerful crystals.

Long ago, in the early times, in the days when the earth was young, the sun became angry with the people. She thought that they were being rude to her, because when they looked at her, they screwed up their faces. So she sent down sultry rays and made them sick with fever. Many people died. The people didn't know what to do.

They went to the Little Men, Anisgaya-Tsunsdiga, the Thunder Boys, for help.

"There's only one thing to do," said the wildest of the two brothers. "You have to kill her before she kills all of you."

The people had no idea how to kill the sun, so the Little Men turned two of them into snakes, a copperhead and a spreading adder.

"Every day in the middle of the day," said the wild Thunder Boy, "the sun stops for a rest and a meal at her daughter's house just in the middle of the Sky Vault. Go up there and wait, and when she arrives, strike her and kill her."

So the two snakes who had been men went to the house of the daughter of the sun and waited. When the sun came close, the spreading adder prepared to strike, but he was blinded by the brilliance of the sun. He closed his eyes and opened his mouth and spit out yellow slime, and that's all he can do to this day.

"Go away, you nasty worm," said the sun.

The copperhead was disgusted at the behavior of his companion. He didn't even try. Both snakes crawled away, their task undone.

The Thunder Boys selected two more men who were willing to try to kill the sun to save the people. They made one into a rattlesnake, and the other they made Ukitena, Keen-eyed. The *uk'ten'* was a monster snake, as big around as a tree trunk. Horns grew on his head, and he had wings. On his forehead between his eyes was a blazing crystal called *uluhnsadi*, transparent. The dazzling light from the crystal was nearly blinding, and its blinding light would so confuse anyone who looked at it that he would run directly toward it. And the *uk'ten'* can kill with a look or with his fetid breath. The Thunder Boys were proud of the *uk'ten'*, and the people were all afraid. Surely this monster would kill the sun.

The next day, the *uk'ten'* and the rattlesnake headed for the house of the daughter of the sun to lie in wait. The *uk'ten'* tried his wings. He was enjoying his flight, and he took his time, but the rattlesnake hurried on ahead. It was almost time for the sun to arrive, and the rattlesnake was coiled up in front of the door, waiting to strike. The door opened, and the rattlesnake struck, but it was the daughter of the sun looking out to see if her mother was coming. She fell down in the door—dead. The rattlesnake raced away just as the *uk'ten'* arrived. When the *uk'ten'* saw what the rattlesnake had done, he became very angry, and he, too, left.

As the days went by, the *uk'ten'* grew more angry, and he became dangerous to the people, so the Thunder Boys sent him away. They sent him up above the Sky Vault to live, but before he went, he left behind many others, images of himself, and they hide in lonely mountain passes and in deep pools in the river.

And the *uk'ten'* wasn't the only danger in deep water. Like-a-Pumpkin thought about the man who had turned into a great water snake because he had violated a food tabu. There could be many like him. That sort of thing must have happened often. He thought of the *dakwa*, the giant fish that could swallow a man. A man had once escaped from a *dakwa* after having been swallowed. He had found mussel shells in the *dakwa*'s belly, and he had used one for a knife and sliced his way out, but the juices in the *dakwa*'s stomach caused all of the man's hair to fall out, and he was bald for the rest of his life. Then there was the great leech the size of a house. It was said that he left the bodies of men lying about with their noses and ears eaten

off. If people got too near the water where the great leech
lived, the water itself would rise up and sweep them in,
and then the leech could get them. And there were the
water cannibals, but Like-a-Pumpkin was not particularly
worried about them. They didn't attack people in the water. They sneaked out of the river in the early hours of the
morning to kill people in their beds and eat them. And
there was yet another worry. Like-a-Pumpkin could not
swim.

His fears of what might be lurking beneath him in the
deep waters did not leave him until he felt the bottom of
the boat scrape ground on the opposite side of the river.
The priests disembarked, said their thanks and farewells
with nods, smiles and gestures, picked up their bundles
and staffs and started walking west. The naked oarsmen
waved at them until they were almost out of sight, then
shoved their canoes back into the water, pointed back toward home.

As the priests walked on, Like-a-Pumpkin, who did not
like leaving a story unfinished, even in his own mind, hurriedly skimmed over the rest of the tale he had abandoned
at the western bank of the river. He reminded himself of
how, when the sun arrived and found her daughter dead,
she went into the house to mourn, and she refused to
come out again. The earth was covered in darkness, and it
became like an endless night. The people went again to
the Thunder Boys for help.

"You'll have to bring her daughter back," they said.
"That's the only way."

They selected seven men for the task and gave each
man a sourwood rod. Then they gave the men a box with
a lid.

"This is to carry her in," they said.

They told the men to go to the Darkening Land, Usun-hiyi, far to the west. Once there, they would have to find Tsusginai, the Ghost Country, and there they would find the daughter of the sun.

"Each man must strike her with his rod," they said. "Then she will fall down in a swoon. Put her in the box and bring her back to her house. Then the sun will be happy again, and everything will be all right. But no matter what happens, don't take the lid off the box until you're back at her house."

The seven men found the Darkening Land and the Ghost Country, and they saw the ghosts all having a dance. They went up close to watch, and the ghosts did not seem to notice. The daughter of the sun was dancing around the circle on the outer edge. As she passed by the men, the first one struck her with his rod. She gave him a curious look and then danced on. When she came around again, the second man struck her, and each man struck her in turn until she made her seventh circle and was touched by the seventh rod. Then she fell in a swoon. The men picked her up and put her inside the box. They put the lid on tight and started for her home.

Along the way she began to cry to be let out, and the men ignored her, but her cries grew more pitiful, and one man began to feel sorry for her.

"I'm hungry," she said.

They went on, and she continued to cry, until they were very near her house, and the man could stand it no longer. He lifted the lid, and out she flew with a flutter of wings, the daughter of the sun, transformed, a redbird.

Then Like-a-Pumpkin asked himself, was Thunder's house, their destination, in the Darkening Land? Was it near the Ghost Country? Would they, if they went that

far, encounter the original *uk'ten'*? He remembered too
late his earlier resolve not to think of such things, to con-
centrate instead on more immediate perils, for as they
followed a trail which led them between high boulders on
either side, screaming men leaped down upon them.

Fourteen

LIKE-A-PUMPKIN screamed out loud in spite of himself as the fearful figure of a painted warrior dropped to the ground just in front of his face. The man wore only a breechclout with tassels and moccasins. His hair grew long, to below his waist, and his face was painted half red, half black. Like-a-Pumpkin turned to run, but the man grabbed him from behind and grappled him to the ground. He knew that other men had jumped Water Moccasin and Deadwood Lighter, but he was too busy defending himself to see what else was happening. His ears were filled with the sounds of scuffling, of blows and of hideous shrieks. The man on top of him was pummeling his face, so Like-a-Pumpkin, having already dropped his bundle and his staff, covered his face with both his arms in an attempt to ward off the blows.

At last the attacker, realizing that he was meeting with little resistance, ceased his blows and stood up, dragging Like-a-Pumpkin along to his feet. The others were all standing by then, and Like-a-Pumpkin and his two companions were shoved together and surrounded by the fierce strangers. One of the strangers, green lines painted on his face, reached around behind the mostly shaved head of Water Moccasin to grab the long, loose hanging scalplock at the back. He pulled Water Moccasin's head back and with the obsidian bladed knife in his other hand, approached the stretched, exposed neck. The warrior with the black and red face paint spoke sharply, and a heated discussion followed. Green Stripes grudgingly released Water Moccasin and stepped back. Apparently, Black and Red had won the argument.

They walked the rest of that day surrounded, carefully watched and often prodded along their way by their captors. At dusk the strangers stopped to camp. They made Deadwood Lighter gather firewood, Water Moccasin build the fire and Like-a-Pumpkin cook. Because their orders were not always readily understood, they were often emphasized by blows. Like-a-Pumpkin found only one decent quality to note about the fierce strangers. They fed their captives as well as they fed themselves. But their kindness, if it was that, ended there, so Like-a-Pumpkin decided that kindness, after all, had nothing to do with it. They intended to keep up the strength of their captives in order to be able to make them work and so that they would be able to keep up on the trail. He wondered where these painted creatures lived and how far they would take them.

When the meal was done, the painted men jerked the priests to their feet again and stripped them of their robes. They took the bundles the priests had carried and opened them. Black and Red found Like-a-Pumpkin's folded pages.

"Be careful of that," Like-a-Pumpkin shouted, reaching out frantically toward the journal, his sacred charge. Green Stripes struck him hard across the back, knocking him to his knees there before Black and Red. Black and Red gave Like-a-Pumpkin a vicious kick to the ribs, and Like-a-Pumpkin doubled over. After that he did not know from whom the blows came, but he felt certain that he would be beaten to death. Then they stopped. Like-a-Pumpkin crawled back over beside his traveling companions, now fellow captives. He looked up. Black and Red was turning the bark pages this way and that, examining them with curiosity and impatience. His lips twisted into a cruel smile as he looked down on Like-a-Pumpkin. Then he casually tossed the bark into the fire, and the painted men all laughed.

Like-a-Pumpkin did not die. He even surprised himself by sleeping well that night, although he did suffer some frightening dreams. In the morning they ate again, and then they resumed their journey. Like-a-Pumpkin noted that they were traveling southwest. The walk was painful for him because of the beating he had suffered the night before, but the sharp initial pains had subsided into dull aches, and he had time to think about the tremendous loss of not only the text he had thus far produced, but also his writing materials.

They stopped to eat again when the sun was almost directly overhead, at her daughter's house, thought Like-a-Pumpkin, but there is no daughter there. The mountains, or hills, around them by this time were much smaller than those which Like-a-Pumpkin was used to at home. They were still covered with thick woods. Again the three captives were made to do the work of the camp and the meal. Like-a-Pumpkin noticed that each captive seemed to have become the property of one individual from the group of fierce strangers. Black and Red seemed to have laid claim to Like-a-Pumpkin, Green Stripes to Water Moccasin, and a man with the bottom half of his face painted yellow to Deadwood Lighter. Somehow that development and the knowledge of it made life easier. No one but Black and Red would order Like-a-Pumpkin to do something, and no one else would beat him. Like-a-Pumpkin had also had time to count his captors. There were eight of them.

Edohi had not seen a Shawnee village that day he had started up the mountain. He had slept that night on the slope before reaching the mountain crest. The next day, he made it to the summit by the time the sun was directly overhead, and he ate lightly from his supply of parched corn, then started the descent on the other side. That was when he saw the village. He was pleased with himself that his judgment had been correct. It had simply been a little farther along the trail than he had guessed it would be. He was on the side of a tree-covered mountain overlooking a river valley. The village below was between the river and the base of the mountain. There was no fence around the village. The houses were small and bark-covered, and there were only about twenty of them. Edohi reasoned that the village was probably a fairly new one, established by people who had moved away from a town that had grown too large. He started down the mountain, moving slowly and cautiously. It took him most of the rest of that day to locate a suitable spot, one close enough to see the people in the village clearly, yet still high enough to allow for a wide view, clear enough for his sightlines, yet providing cover for himself. He settled down there for the night.

The next day and half of the next, Edohi waited and

watched. Then he located his prey. A man alone left the village. From his distance, Edohi estimated him to be a young man, his own age perhaps, perhaps a little older. He was a tall man, handsome and well proportioned. He wore only moccasins and leggings with a breechclout and some decorative jewelry, arm bands, a necklace of some kind, baubles all along the edges of both ears. His head was shaved, and his scalplock, growing out of the top of his head, flowed loosely down his back, similar to Edohi's own. He carried a bow, a quiver of arrows, a wooden, ball-headed warclub and a knife. He was not painted. He was going hunting, Edohi surmised.

He left the village by the road, and, conveniently for Edohi, he headed south. Edohi kept the man in sight as much as possible and followed him. He'd have to plan his moves carefully. The man was alone, but so was Edohi, and the Shawnee looked to Edohi as if he would make a formidable foe indeed. Edohi was not afraid to fight any man, but this time he meant to win, and he meant to take this man alive, unhurt if possible. He would have to plan carefully, watch for any opportunities and be prepared for action at any time.

Like-a-Pumpkin tried to think positive thoughts. He and his companions were the captives of some strange, ferocious people, and he had lost his writing implements, but they were still alive, and they were still headed, generally, in the right direction. Their captors were taking them farther south than they would have gone on their own, but they were also traveling west, and more west than south. Somewhere along the way, they would see their chance to escape, and then they would resume their own journey. Not too much time would have been lost. The thought of his mission and its importance, not only to the Real People, but also to all of their close neighbors, gave him strength and the will to endure. His cuts and bruises still ached, but the pain was not unbearable. He walked on, carrying the bundle of odds and ends that Black and Red had thrust at him earlier in the day.

The trail they walked wound its way through a thick woods, and Like-a-Pumpkin noticed that it had begun to parallel a fast-running brook. Then abruptly the trail took them out of the woods into a small clearing, and there in the middle of the clearing, beside the brook, was a squalid camp. It must be a camp, Like-a-Pumpkin thought. It couldn't be the actual village of these people.

Women and children shouted and ran toward the returning warriors. Dogs barked and ran in circles. The camp itself, or village, consisted of a dozen or so small conical dwellings, tents really, constructed by the covering over of a stack of poles with scraps of skin. There was a tremendous amount of noise and activity for a place so small, Like-a-Pumpkin thought, and then he noticed the stench. It came upon him and sickened him, the overwhelming odor of human and animal waste, of a variety of skins in various stages of processing, of unwashed human bodies in close proximity on a sweltering summer day. Flies and gnats swarmed.

And the people swarmed. They swarmed around the captives, curious. They looked. They touched and poked. Like-a-Pumpkin had grown used to being naked with his captors on the trail, but here in this wretched camp surrounded by all these strange and curious people, men, women and children, he suddenly felt newly stripped and humiliated.

The initial excitement and its accompanying flurry of activity subsided, and Black and Red pushed Like-a-Pumpkin ahead of him to one of the sorry tents. A woman followed them. Black and Red's wife, Like-a-Pumpkin thought. Black and Red tied Like-a-Pumpkin's wrists together behind his back with a long piece of rawhide rope. The other end he tied to a stake which was driven into the ground there in front of the tent. Then Black and Red and his woman went inside the smelly tent. Like-a-Pumpkin stood naked, alone and self-conscious. He stood for a moment, then decided that he had been temporarily abandoned, left to himself at last, and he squatted beside the stake. A moment later he sat on the ground and started to look around the camp.

Most of the people seemed to have already forgotten about him. A few still stared. Off to his right he could see Water Moccasin similarly tied in front of another hovel. Green Stripes was there with two women. They seemed to be arguing. Then Green Stripes knocked Water Moccasin to the ground with a vicious blow and ducked inside the tent. The two women went back to whatever it was they had been doing before. Like-a-Pumpkin couldn't tell for sure from where he sat, but they seemed to be scraping a hide of some kind. He looked around some more, but he couldn't locate Deadwood Lighter.

It was evening, and soon the village women were busy preparing food. Like-a-Pumpkin was released and made to carry firewood, and he managed to accomplish his task with a minimum number of blows from Black and Red and his woman. He noticed, though, that Water Moccasin was not faring so well. Green Stripes and his two women kept shouting angrily at Water Moccasin and beating him unmercifully. Like-a-Pumpkin figured that Water Moccasin was not understanding their demands and, therefore, not responding quickly enough to suit them. He felt sorry for Water Moccasin, but he was too busy catering to the demands of his own tormentors to think about much else.

He did wonder still about the whereabouts and the welfare of Deadwood Lighter.

Like-a-Pumpkin was again well fed, and he was not bothered again that evening. He was tied to the stake for the night and left to sleep alone, naked on the bare ground in front of the tent. He was just as glad. He thought that the stench and the pesky insects and the barely tolerable heat would be even worse inside than out. He felt filthy and dropped off to sleep longing for a bath in clear, swift-running water.

At dawn, Like-a-Pumpkin was released and taken to the edge of the woods where Black and Red made it clear to him that he was once again to gather firewood. He noticed that Water Moccasin had been assigned the same task by Green Stripes. As the two captives worked their way along the edge of the clearing selecting just the right sticks, they found themselves close together, bending over to pick up sticks. Like-a-Pumpkin glanced up from his work, and his eyes made brief contact with those of Water Moccasin.

"Like-a-Pumpkin," said Water Moccasin in a harsh whisper, "we must escape. Now is our chance."

"But where is Deadwood Lighter?" Like-a-Pumpkin asked.

"I don't know where he is. We can't wait for him. We have to get ourselves out of here."

"I don't know," said Like-a-Pumpkin. "They can all see us right now."

"We can outrun them," said Water Moccasin. "This may be our only chance."

Like-a-Pumpkin looked at Water Moccasin, and his heart was pounding. He felt himself begin to tremble. But Water Moccasin looked totally frantic. His eyes were wild. His face and body were covered with cuts and bruises.

"We have our mission to accomplish," said Water Moccasin, his voice rising with frustration and anger.

Just then one of Green Stripes's women kicked Water Moccasin in the side, knocking him to the ground. He landed on his belly, falling on the pile of jagged sticks he had gathered. She shouted some sort of recriminations at the sprawling, naked priest and kicked at him again, but this time Water Moccasin grabbed her by the ankle and flung her to the ground. She shrieked, as he scrambled to his feet, scooped up the pile of sticks he had gathered and dropped, and tossed them at her. Then he ran.

"Come on, Like-a-Pumpkin," he shouted. "Come on."

The woman kicked and flailed at the sticks and angrily spewed forth words in her strange language. Like-a-Pumpkin stood frozen with fear. He watched with a terrible fascination as Water Moccasin ran, not into the woods just there where they had been working, but across the clearing, toward the thicket on the other side. Black and Red shouted something, and his woman came running from their tent, carrying Black and Red's long bow and a few arrows. The distance from the tent to where Black and Red stood waiting was only about a fourth of that across the clearing, and Water Moccasin was still in full view in the open as Black and Red coldly nocked an arrow and pulled back on the string. Like-a-Pumpkin stood horrified as he watched his companion run for his life, watched Black and Red calmly release the string, saw the arrow fly, then strike its mark with a sickening thud, driving itself into the bare back of Water Moccasin. Water Moccasin tumbled in the dry grass and lay still, and Like-a-Pumpkin knew that he was dead.

A chaos of noise and activity followed. Like-a-Pumpkin

was grabbed by several arms and pushed into the center of the camp, and then at last he saw Deadwood Lighter, for others had done the same with him. Then the beatings started. They were pounded by men, women and children with sticks, hands and rawhide ropes. They were beaten until they collapsed on the ground. They were kicked, and again Like-a-Pumpkin was sure that he would be beaten to death. But at last the beating stopped, and Deadwood Lighter was dragged off somewhere while Black and Red took Like-a-Pumpkin back to the edge of the clearing to finish his chore. He was afraid that he would not be able to accomplish the task, but he knew that if he failed to do so, he would be punished more. So he gathered the wood, slowly and painfully, and he carried it to Black and Red's tent. Then he was again bound and tied to the stake.

He figured that he and Deadwood Lighter had been beaten as a warning to them not to try what Water Moccasin had tried, although he thought that what had happened to Water Moccasin should have been warning enough. The killing of Water Moccasin had stunned him, and the beating had quickly followed, but sitting quietly and alone, albeit in considerable pain, he had time to reflect. The awful reality began to overcome the mind and body of Like-a-Pumpkin, and he began to shudder with silent sobs. He took deep breaths, trying to regain control of his own muscles, but as he lifted his head to suck in some of the putrid air around him, he saw the body of Water Moccasin lying neglected where it had fallen, the missile of death still protruding from its back. Just then a scruffy-looking dog crept slowly into his view. It looked around itself, cowering as it moved, as if it expected to be hit or kicked at any moment. No one bothered it. It reached its destination, and it began to sniff tentatively at the body lying there. Like-a-Pumpkin dropped his head into his arms.

He had to find a way to escape, but it would not be Water Moccasin's way. He had to find a way that would work. Water Moccasin had made several mistakes, fatal ones. First he had spoken to Like-a-Pumpkin. That had drawn attention to him. Like-a-Pumpkin resolved right then that he would think only of himself, and he hoped that Deadwood Lighter would have the good sense to do the same. Then Water Moccasin had acted spontaneously, without planning, and he had made his break in the light of day in full view of his captors. It had been foolish, stupid, and Like-a-Pumpkin could only think that his unfortunate fellow-priest had acted in response to a moment of panic. His mind must have been distracted. Perhaps, he thought, I would have done the same had I been subjected to the treatment of Green Stripes and his nasty women. Finally poor Water Moccasin had run the wrong direction and had made himself an easy target, again, Like-a-Pumpkin figured, as a result of panic and confusion.

Like-a-Pumpkin silently and solemnly resolved to endure whatever torments and whatever humiliation his captors might devise until the time was right. He resolved that he would live to return to the land of the Real People.

Fifteen

NOT EVERYONE was there, but each of the
seven clans was represented, as were most of the
individual households of Ijodi. There were even visitors
from other towns. It was not an official gathering. It had
not been planned. A few people had been lounging about
around the townhouse, talking and smoking, just passing
the time. The discussion had gradually become more serious, more heated, and more people had joined in. The
word had spread that a meeting was in progress, and others had hurried to the townhouse, afraid that they might
be missing out on something important. What had started
out as casual conversation had evolved into a full-blown
town meeting. The topic was the *Ani-Kutani.* Corn
Flower sat quietly listening as Big Bear, the father of
Edohi, spoke.

"They are taking too much power to themselves," he
said. "Their charge is the conduct of our ceremonies, but
they have taken over our lives. We've seen it coming for

several years now, but we did nothing about it. We let it happen."

"What could we have done?" someone asked.

"Big Bear is right," said Hemp Carrier. "The *Ani-Kutani* have become too powerful, and they misuse their powers. They have even changed the old stories, some of them."

"How do you know that?"

"When I was a small child," said Big Bear, "I remember my grandfather telling of a long migration of the Real People. He said that the Real People lived on an island far to the south of here. They were attacked on that island, he said, by warriors from seventy different tribes of people, and that was too many, even for the Real People. They fled the island and traveled to the big coast in boats. Then they walked north for a long time. They walked so far north, they came to a land that was cold almost all of the time. They went east from there, and then they fought with the *Ani-Senika*, the *Ani-Skalali* and all the other *Ani-nuhdawegi*. Then the *Aquanuhgis* joined in the fight against the Real People, and they moved south again. But not so far south as the place they had come from originally. They stopped at this place and settled here."

"That's right," said Hemp Carrier. "I, too, recall that tale. The first town they built here was Kituwah. Therefore we sometimes call ourselves *Ani-Kituwah*, Kituwah People."

"But what does that mean?" someone asked. "Kituwah People?"

"I don't know," said Hemp Carrier.

"The priests know," said Big Bear, "and they won't tell us. They keep their secrets."

"But you said the stories have been changed," protested a young man sitting on a bench at the front of the crowd.

"Don't you know the tale they tell us now about our origin?" said Hemp Carrier. "They say that the world was created for us right here. This land was made for us when Dayunisi, Beaver's Grandchild, the little water beetle, brought the mud up from beneath the waters and spread it out on the surface of the water. Then Suli, the Great Buzzard, flew over the mud flapping his giant wings to dry it out. When he flew low, he created valleys with the downward motion of his wings and hills with their upward sweep. The valleys and hills right here around us."

"If we came from a place far to the south and across the water," said Big Bear, "how can it also be that this place was made for us in the beginning? That this is the place our first ancestors came to when they came down from on top of the Sky Vault?"

"They've changed the stories," an old man said, solemnly nodding his head. "I thought that I was the only one left who remembered. I thought no one cared anymore."

"And still there is no rain," shouted the Spoiler. "Our crops are withering, and our streams and rivers are drying up. What good is the power of the priests, what good their keeping of our ceremonies and their secrets if they cannot bring us the rain?"

Corn Flower thought about Two Heads. His behavior and his arrogant attitude were certainly not priest-like. Perhaps, she thought, these people are right. The *Ani-Kutani* have overreached their rightful authority. If that were not the case, how could one like Two Heads be given the status of *kutani?* She had not told anyone, not even her mother, the Spoiler, of the unpleasant episode with Two Heads by the river. She kept it to herself, and during the discussion about the priests there in the Ijodi townhouse, she still kept quiet. Her mother, she thought, had voice enough for them both, and the issues should be kept general. The power of the priests was the topic, not the personality of Two Heads.

"I have heard that some of them can make picture-talk," a woman said. "Surely that is sorcery."

"What we're doing here," said another, "talking about these things, is dangerous. The gods will be angry with us."

"Questioning the authority of the *Ani-Kutani*," said Hemp Carrier, "is not the same thing as questioning the authority of the gods, even though the *Ani-Kutani* would like for us to think it so."

The meeting broke up much as it had begun, slowly and informally. Nothing was resolved. No suggestions for action had even been made. The bold talk stopped short of even proposing that the concerns of the people be somehow conveyed to the priests. No one, it seemed, was ready to go to that extreme. Corn Flower walked alone for a time after she left the townhouse. She wondered if the events of the day made any sense at all. All she had learned was that almost everyone in Ijodi was unhappy with the present situation. Almost everyone questioned the authority and the motives and the powers of the priests. Almost everyone was afraid.

Edohi followed the Shawnee all day. The man simply walked the trail going south. At midday he had stopped to eat a light meal. Then he had continued on his way. A few times Edohi lost sight of his quarry, for he was traveling through the trees and along the mountainside in order to keep his presence a secret. That night the Shawnee camped beside the road. Edohi considered attacking the man in his sleep, but he rejected that idea. A fight between the two of them could be furious, and one of them might be seriously hurt or even killed. That would not accomplish Edohi's purpose. He decided that he, too, would sleep.

But sleep did not come easy that night for Edohi. Many things were on his mind, and the thoughts tumbled around in his head keeping him long awake. He tried to keep foremost in his mind the immediate task he had set for himself, the job of successfully stalking and eventually capturing the Shawnee. And it was important to Edohi that he accomplish this feat without seriously injuring the Shawnee. He wanted to present his captive whole and healthy to the Spoiler. If she should choose to maim, torture, even kill the Shawnee, that would be her business, her choice.

As important and immediate as all that was to Edohi, he couldn't keep himself from thinking ahead, from dreaming about, fantasizing about the hoped-for fruits of his labor. He considered the beauty of Corn Flower and dared to imagine her secret, private charms and to hope that they would be his. It was hard for Edohi to believe that this girl who had been his lifelong playmate and friend now seemed to him almost to be a mysterious stranger.

He tried to imagine what life would be like for him with Corn Flower for his wife, but aside from ambiguous images of night pleasures, he could only recall innocent, joyous scenes from the past, scenes of running together in the mountains, swimming in the clear streams, hunting.

And then he wondered if the cold, clear streams would all dry up. Some of the smaller ones were already dry. As he lay there, not really thinking, rather being kept awake by these thoughts, the air was hot and dry and still, even though the sun was long gone to the other side of the Sky Vault. It seemed to Edohi that the night was as hot as the day had been. Even the absence of the sun had not brought relief. Was it the heat, the dry, oppressive heat that was keeping him awake, or was it the thoughts?

He was awake at dawn. The sun had only just appeared at the eastern edge of the Sky Vault. Edohi sat up and stretched. He glanced down toward the camp of the Shawnee, and he stood up with a start. The man was gone. Edohi chastised himself for having slept so late. He gathered his few belongings and started to run down the slope to the road, but he stopped himself. Suppose the man had not yet gone far. Or maybe he had somehow discovered that he was being followed. Edohi would be foolish to rush ahead, not knowing what might be awaiting him.

He moved slowly down to the road and, keeping himself well hidden, watched for a while. He saw nothing and heard nothing. Cautiously, he moved out into the road and across to the site of the Shawnee's camp. Tracks indicated that the man had left, still going south, still on the road. Edohi followed. He thought that it would be safe enough for him to stay on the road for a little while, long enough to catch up with the Shawnee. When he arrived at the first bend in the road, the first spot where he had no clear view of the road ahead, he stopped, moved to the edge and eased around the bend. Still he saw no one, so he continued on the road.

The sun was halfway up to her daughter's house when Edohi saw that the Shawnee's tracks left the road going toward the river. The woods were thick off the road on both sides, and Edohi had a moment of indecision. He had no idea where the man might be. He could try to follow the tracks, but in the dense growth, he could be as surprised as his prey if he happened on him unexpectedly. He crossed the road and started to climb the mountain again. It was well past midday by the time he gave up trying to find a place that would afford him a good view of the river. He went back down to the road, back across to the river side and, north of where the Shawnee had left the road, into the woods. By the time he reached the river, the day was almost done. He sat down in the cover of the trees and ate the last of his parched corn. Then, carefully looking around, he moved down to the water's edge and drank deeply of the cold, clear water. He decided that he would resume his search with the first light of day.

He had just settled down for the night when he saw the smoke, a thin wisp rising to just above the treetops before dissipating in the graying sky. A campfire. The man had made a camp for the night. Edohi glanced toward the Sky Vault and said a word of thanks. Then he stood up and started walking south along the riverbank. He stopped for a moment when he saw the flickering light of the small fire, then moved ahead slowly until he could see clearly the outline of the man sitting there alone, eating. He squatted down to watch and to think.

Should he wait until morning, he wondered, or should he attack? He would be well rested in the morning, but so would his enemy. And waiting until morning, he would run the risk of repeating his mistake of the previous night, sleeping later than his prey. He did not want to injure the man. He wanted to present the Spoiler with a healthy Shawnee slave. Yet he could think of no way to proceed other than by direct confrontation. And the time, he decided, would never be better than the present. He crept in the shadows until he was as close to the camp as he felt he could get without giving himself away. He carefully laid aside his bow and arrows, gave a hitch to the rawhide rope around his waist, gripped his warclub firmly in his right hand and stood up. He saw no reaction from the Shawnee. He took three long, bold steps away from the cover of the woods, toward the river. Still the man did not react. Edohi walked toward the camp, expecting the man to leap to his feet, but he did not. About six paces from the fire, Edohi stopped. The Shawnee slowly raised his head and looked across the flames at Edohi.

"You're *Allegewi*," he said, speaking perfectly in the language of the Real People but using the Shawnee and Delaware name for them. "You've been following me. I wondered when you'd show yourself. Have you come to kill me?"

"You speak my language," said Edohi.

"Yes. And five or six others. Did you come to kill me?"

"No," said Edohi. "I came to take you captive."

The Shawnee shook his head slowly.

"I won't go," he said. "Not without a fight. If you simply wanted to kill me, I wouldn't resist, but I won't submit to captivity without a fight. What's your name?"

Edohi hesitated a moment, puzzled by the Shawnee's talk, his strange attitude.

"My name?" he said. "Why do you ask?"

"We're going to fight," said the Shawnee. "I want to know who I'm fighting, who might kill me, or who it is that I might kill. I'm called Man Alone, or He-Who-Has-Been-Kicked-Out, or the Outcast. You choose. It's a new name, but it's the only one I carry now. What are you called?"

"I'm called Edohi. I saw you leave your village. I thought you were going hunting."

"No. I left for good."

"Why?" Edohi asked.

"I've been disgraced, and my own people, those who used to be my people, shun me. I led some men north on a raid, and three were killed. But enough talk, Edohi," said the Outcast, standing upright, his own warclub in hand. "Will you kill me now? I'm ready to die."

"I want you alive," said Edohi.

"Then try to take me."

The Outcast sprang across the fire, his club held high. Edohi stepped aside just in time to avoid a deadly blow. Both men quickly turned to face each other. They circled. Then the Outcast swung his club again. Edohi stepped aside, dropped his own club, clasped his hands together, and brought them down hard across the Shawnee's back. The Outcast fell forward, sprawling in the dirt. Edohi threw himself at the man's back, but the Outcast rolled aside just in time. Edohi was on his face on the ground. The Outcast raised his club high and, aiming for the back of Edohi's head, brought it down with all the strength of his right arm. Edohi turned onto his back as the stone-headed club smashed into the earth just beside his head, grazing his face, burning a line across his left cheekbone. He shouted out in pain as he grabbed the Outcast's wrist with both his hands and, twisting the arm, stood up. But the Outcast was on his feet, too, and he moved quickly behind Edohi, reaching around Edohi's throat with his left arm. Edohi still held the Shawnee's right wrist, but his own breath was being cut off by the stranglehold. He was being pulled backward, off balance, and he was choking. He worked his right leg between the legs of the Outcast and jerked it forward, at the same time flinging his own weight back. They hit the ground hard, but Edohi landed on top, knocking the wind out of the Outcast's lungs. The death grip around Edohi's throat relaxed, and he rolled free. Moving quickly, he turned the Outcast over. In an instant, Edohi was on the man's back, twisting an arm behind him.

"Now you're my prisoner," said Edohi.

"Yes," said the Outcast, beginning to get back his breath, "for just as long as you sit on my back. Unless you kill me now, I'll fight you again when I get up."

Edohi looked down at the rope which was wrapped around his waist. He tried to figure out how he could hold the Outcast down with one hand and with the other get the rope loose from around his waist and then tie the Outcast's hands behind his back. There was no way. The Outcast had dropped his warclub when the two men had last struggled to their feet. It lay on the ground to Edohi's right, an arm's length away. He reached for it, clutched it, raised it overhead, hesitated an instant, then brought it down with a thud. The Outcast went limp beneath him. Edohi pulled the man's hands together behind his back and tied them tight. He hoped that he was not tying the hands of a dead man.

Sixteen

WILD HEMP visited with the Spoiler, and Hemp Carrier went to see Stinging Ant. They talked about the dry weather and the poor crops. They complained about the *Ani-Kutani*. They reminisced about old times, and they talked about Corn Flower and Edohi. The talk was general and roundabout, and it was all pleasant.

The next few days they gathered things together from among the people of the Bird Clan, Edohi's clan, and when they thought that they had enough, they wrapped it in the hide of *yansa*, the buffalo, and carried it to the Spoiler: pots, shell gorgets, baskets of honeysuckle and river cane splints and oak splints, intricate pottery stamps, beautifully tanned deer hides, woven floor mats, and blankets, bags and cloth woven from fiber of bark, flax, hemp, nettles and grasses and dyed in a variety of colors and designs. At the same time, other Bird People made gifts to others in the Deer Clan. The Spoiler and the others accepted their gifts, and again the Spoiler talked with Wild

Hemp. No clear statements were made, no promises or commitments, yet they seemed to agree. The Spoiler casually mentioned that she was planning to pay a visit to old Gone-in-the-Water, the conjurer, then just as casually changed the subject. Wild Hemp knew, though, that the purpose of the Spoiler's visit to the old man would be to ask him for a judgment concerning the proposed match. Gone-in-the-Water would consult his crystal, and it would tell him whether or not Edohi and Corn Flower would be well suited to each other. Wild Hemp went home pleased. Things were progressing smoothly.

Like-a-Pumpkin was dreaming of rain, torrents of rain pouring down on the thirsty land. He was standing naked on top of the temple mound at Men's Town, looking up into the sky, his eyes squinted, his mouth opened, his arms outstretched, and the rains kept coming. The lush drops beat his flesh, melded together and cascaded over his body. His mouth was filled and running over with the sweet-tasting water. Then a rude kick to his bare buttocks woke him up.

He was lying in the dirt, tied to a stake by a leash. He was hot and dirty and sticky with sweat. There was no rain. There was no sign of rain. Black and Red pulled him to his feet by the rope, untied him and pointed to the remains of the fire and then to the edge of the woods. Like-a-Pumpkin went to gather sticks. He noticed that the firewood was getting scarce around the edge of the clearing, and now and then he had to reach into the woods to pick up a nice fallen branch. He also noticed that Black and Red had followed him and was armed with his bow and arrows. He thought that in another day or so it would be necessary to go farther into the woods to gather sticks, and perhaps that would afford him an opportunity to escape. He heard a grumbling voice, and he looked up from his chore to see one of the women from Green Stripes's tent, also gathering wood. She gave him a hard, menacing look and went on angrily with her work.

When the fire was again low and the morning meal was done, Like-a-Pumpkin, having carried water from the stream, which was getting lower with each passing day and had become murky from overuse, was once again tied to his leash. He heard angry voices coming from the hovel of Green Stripes and his women, and he looked in that direction. The women seemed all to be talking at once. They shouted and gesticulated wildly. Now and then Green Stripes interjected a bark into the general uproar, but his barks seemed to have no effect. Then Like-a-Pumpkin noticed that one of the women, the one who had been gathering wood that morning, was looking toward him. She pointed at him and shouted something to Green Stripes. Then Green Stripes made a wild gesture of resignation with both his arms and started walking toward Like-a-Pumpkin. As he neared the tent, he shouted something, and Black and Red came out.

There was a brief, calm exchange between the two men, during which Green Stripes occasionally gestured back toward his women, still huddled there in front of their own ragged tent, glaring after their husband. One of them shouted something, and Green Stripes waved an arm backward at her impatiently, a motion Like-a-Pumpkin interpreted as meant to shush her. Green Stripes continued talking to Black and Red. Now and then he either glanced at or pointed toward Like-a-Pumpkin, sitting there on the ground. Then Like-a-Pumpkin realized to his horror that he was the subject of this debate. He instinctively hugged his knees closer to his chest, just as Green Stripes punctuated a sentence by pointing a long arm toward the remains of poor Water Moccasin, still lying where they had fallen, and Like-a-Pumpkin thought that he then understood the whole discussion.

Obviously the wives of Green Stripes were grumbling about the work they had to do since Black and Red had killed their slave. The present argument must be, he thought, that Black and Red should give them Like-a-Pumpkin to replace the one he had killed. Like-a-Pumpkin imagined the rest of the argument, taking both sides in his own mind. If Black and Red had not shot his arrow, Water Moccasin would have run away, and the result would have been the same. Green Stripes's women would have no slave. But no. If Black and Red had not killed the man, they could have chased him and recaptured him. He was alone, naked, unarmed and in unfamiliar territory. Yes, but there was a chance that he might have made it, and if he had, his success would have encouraged the others to try the same thing. It was best to just shoot him as an example. But it always came back to this: Black and Red had killed their slave. Therefore Black and Red owed them a slave, and he should replace him. With Like-a-Pumpkin. Then Black and Red said something with a tone of finality. Green Stripes appeared to be satisfied, and Like-a-Pumpkin felt panic well up inside himself.

Black and Red pulled the end of the leash off the stake and handed it to Green Stripes. Green Stripes turned to lead his prize home, but Black and Red said something else. Green Stripes stopped. He seemed to be considering something, mulling something over in his head. He made a short response, and Black and Red gave a broad smile and ducked back inside his tent. A moment later he reemerged with something clutched in his fist, and Green Stripes pushed Like-a-Pumpkin to the ground. Black and Red sat down cross-legged in the dirt, and Green Stripes sat facing him. They smoothed the dirt between them with the palms of their hands, and Black and Red threw a handful of small round stones out on the ground. Some of them were white and some black. It was some kind of a game, Like-a-Pumpkin thought. A gambling game. So Black and Red had given in on the argument and had allowed Green Stripes to take possession of Like-a-Pumpkin, only to talk the man into gambling with him with Like-a-Pumpkin as the stake. Like-a-Pumpkin said a silent prayer for Black and Red's success. He did not like Black and Red, but the two women over at the tent of Green Stripes filled him with terror.

Like-a-Pumpkin tried to understand the game, but he could not. Just as he thought he had it figured out, something would occur to prove him wrong. Each man tossed the stones several times before the other got his turn, but the number of tosses each man took were not the same from one turn to the next. At the end of a turn, the player would hand the stones over to his opponent and make one or more marks in the dirt beside himself. But just as Like-a-Pumpkin counted up sixteen marks in the dirt beside Black and Red, while Green Stripes had only twelve, Black and Red wiped out all his own marks and started over again with one. Yet, Like-a-Pumpkin thought, that must not have indicated the end of a game, for Green Stripes's twelve marks remained. Like-a-Pumpkin did notice that Black and Red's woman was sitting stoically beside her man, and he saw more than once Green Stripes give her a sideways glance, an evil leer on his face. Had Black and Red bet his wife against Like-a-Pumpkin? It appeared so. The thought was repugnant to Like-a-Pumpkin, but then, everything he knew about these people was horrid. Green Stripes wiped out his marks and started over with one. The game was incomprehensible to

Like-a-Pumpkin, and it seemed interminable, and his fate depended on its outcome.

The Outcast was not dead. After Edohi had bound the man's arms securely behind his back, he had checked the wound. The blow he had delivered to the head had caused a lump and had broken the skin slightly, but Edohi was almost certain he had not cracked bone. He bathed the wound with river water. Then he searched along the edge of the woods until he found the thick web nest of a tiny spider. He stole the nest and plastered it on the Shawnee's head wound. Then he settled down to sleep the night in the camp the Outcast had prepared, one end of the rope which bound his captive's wrists tied to his own right wrist.

He woke up in the early morning light with the sun not yet showing herself above the treetops to find the Shawnee, still securely bound, sitting up and staring with a dull expression into the dead ashes of last night's fire.

"How do you feel?" Edohi said.

"You didn't hit me hard enough," said the Outcast. "I'm still alive."

"I think I hit you just right," said Edohi. He sat for a long moment studying his prisoner. It was the first time he had really been able to take a good look at the man, and he realized that the Shawnee was older than he had thought at first. The man was handsome, and his lithe and supple body had caused Edohi to judge him young. He was older than Edohi, but not so old, Edohi thought, as his own father Big Bear or his uncle Hemp Carrier. Edohi stood up and looked around the camp. He untied the rope end from his own wrist and tied it to a nearby tree trunk. Then he checked the man's supplies and found parched corn and jerked venison. He ate, and he hand-fed his prisoner. The Outcast at first refused the food, but when Edohi tried to force him, he decided that it would be more dignified to accept than to have his captor mash food against his mouth. Finished with the meal, Edohi gave the man a drink of water, then stripped himself and waded into the river. Quietly he gave thanks for his success. The sun was showing herself over the trees by the time Edohi came out of the water, and he let her heat dry his body. He put back on his leggings, breechclout and moccasins. He gathered up his own belongings and those of his captive, and he untied the Shawnee from the tree, leaving his wrists bound behind his back. He took the long rope dangling from the Outcast's wrists up and around the prisoner's neck, then retied the loose end to his own wrist.

"Come on," he said, and they started walking. Edohi led the way back through the woods and out onto the trail. He was headed for home. They walked in silence, Edohi a few steps ahead of his prisoner, the two of them connected by the length of rope. They met no one on the trail. The sun slowly climbed higher, and the day grew hotter. Now and then clouds of gnats swarmed in the path of the travelers, but no clouds were to be seen in the bright blue sky.

"Edohi," said the Outcast.

"What is it?" Edohi asked.

The Outcast walked a little faster, moving abreast of his captor. He walked along beside his captor then for several steps before continuing to speak.

"We have a long walk ahead of us," he said.

"Yes," said Edohi.

"Something could happen along the way."

"I don't think so," said Edohi. "I think you're tightly

tied. I don't believe we'll meet anyone along this way. I don't think anything will happen."

"But you never know, Edohi. On a long walk, something could happen. You may have to kill me yet. Or maybe I'll kill you. Even though you beat me last night, I might win the next time."

"If there is ever a next time," said Edohi.

"Oh, I think that there will be," said the Outcast. "I think that we two will fight again."

The game was over at last. Like-a-Pumpkin could tell by the way in which Black and Red roared his pleasure and by the groan that escaped from the mouth of Green Stripes. Like-a-Pumpkin breathed a heavy sigh of relief as Green Stripes stood, shrugged in resignation and headed back toward his waiting wives. The harangue began before he was halfway back. Both women were scolding at once, and Like-a-Pumpkin wondered why the man could possibly have wanted another to add to his miseries. Behind Green Stripes's back, Black and Red was laughing. Green Stripes shouted angrily and hurried his pace. When he reached the nagging wives, he started swinging his arms, and before he was through, he had knocked them both down and given each one a final kick for good measure. The scolding stopped. Black and Red, still laughing, slapped Like-a-Pumpkin on the shoulder and pointed with his chin toward the tent of Green Stripes. Like-a-Pumpkin ventured a halfhearted, tentative laugh, nodding his agreement with his master. Black and Red laughed even harder, and Like-a-Pumpkin lost control of himself. He joined wholeheartedly in the infectious, raucous laughter of Black and Red. He laughed until tears rolled down his cheeks, and he fell over, rolling naked in the dirt and holding his sides. Black and Red's woman, squatting in the opening of her tent, laughed too.

That night as the camp was going to sleep, Like-a-Pumpkin wept. He thought of his reaction to the outcome of the gambling game. He had been relieved, even overjoyed, and at what? At having been retained as the property of Black and Red. Of course, being owned by Black and Red was much preferable to being owned by Green Stripes and his awful women. Yet his momentary joy illustrated for him the extent of his wretched condition. He had rolled on the ground, naked, laughing hysterically along with his master, a man whose real name he did not even know. He could not understand the language that was being spoken around him, did not know what name to give to these fierce and filthy people. He was like a dog. He was worse off than a dog, for the dogs at least ran free.

Within the range of his vision, the remains of his former companion Water Moccasin lay rotting, unattended and picked over by the camp dogs and other scavengers. His other traveling companion, Deadwood Lighter, was —somewhere. He knew not where. And he himself had been reduced to the lowest imaginable kind of existence. For a moment he thought that Water Moccasin had made the right choice. Death was surely preferable to the lowly existence he was leading. But that morbid thought lasted only a moment, for there was, after all, a third alternative. Escape. Escape and freedom and return to home. He recalled his earlier resolve to bide his time, to wait and watch and endure. The right time would come, and when it did, he would be ready. He would escape. He thought about Jisdu, the rabbit, the great trickster, and how he had escaped from the wolves.

• • • •

The wolves had captured Jisdu, and he knew that if he
didn't think of something soon, they would kill him and
eat him. He started to sing a song, and he started to
dance. The wolves were watching him, curious.

"What are you doing?" they asked.

"It's a new song and a new dance," said Jisdu.

The wolves watched closely, and some of them began
to try to imitate the steps. Then some tried to sing the
words along with Jisdu. He danced a little farther away,
toward the woods. Then all the wolves were singing and
dancing, and Jisdu danced a little farther away. The
wolves danced after him and sang the words to his song.
Jisdu danced closer to the woods; then he suddenly sprang
into the woods and ran away. The wolves followed him,
and one of them picked up his trail. Jisdu found a hollow
tree and climbed up inside, and the wolf came sniffing
along his trail. He sniffed his way up to the hollow tree,
and as he poked his snuffling nose into the hollow, Jisdu
spit in his eyes, and the wolf ran away howling.

Like-a-Pumpkin would have to do more than spit in the
eyes of Black and Red. He knew that. Yet he was in a
clearing and there were woods. Could he sing and dance
his way to the woods? He doubted it. Yet somehow he
knew that in the story of Jisdu and the wolves there was a
lesson for him, a lesson that would apply to his current
predicament. He dropped off to sleep, and he dreamed
about the rabbit's dance, about the song that Jisdu sang
and about escape into the woods.

Ijodi came into view, and Edohi felt his chest swell with
pride. He had captured his Shawnee, and he had brought
him home. He had remained alert, ready for any kind of

trouble, all the long trip home, but there had been none. The Shawnee had not tried to escape, and they had not encountered anyone along the trail. Home at last, his mission accomplished, Edohi relaxed.

"There's my town," he said. "It's called Ijodi. This is the end of our journey. And you see, nothing has happened. We're here, and you're still my captive."

"Now I suppose you'll kill me slowly in front of all your friends," said the Outcast. "Go ahead. I'm not afraid of your tortures. I know how to die."

"I don't know what will happen to you," said Edohi, and he realized that he really didn't, and he felt a pang of guilt. "It's not for me to decide. Come on."

Edohi led his captive on down the road to the entryway into the town. He was met with happy greetings and with cheers from the people who saw him come in.

"Edohi," said one, smiling, "what is that you have there?"

"We thought you'd bring back a deer," said another, "but you've brought a dog. A live one, too."

Their shouts brought others to see what was going on. Soon Edohi, pulling his captive along behind him, found himself in front of the townhouse with just about the entire population of Ijodi gathered around. When the shouting died down, he responded to the demands of the crowd and told the story of how he had captured the Outcast. As he spoke he looked over the crowd. He saw Corn Flower there, and he imagined that he saw pride in her eyes. He found his uncle Hemp Carrier, and he could see the smile on Hemp Carrier's face. Hemp Carrier alone knew why Edohi had done this deed. He saw his own mother, and he saw the Spoiler, and when his tale was told, he walked to the Spoiler and held out the end of the rope toward her.

"I brought this for you," he said, "to help you balance your loss of long ago."

The Spoiler looked into Edohi's eyes, not long enough to be threatening or rude, just enough to read his face. Then she looked hard at the Shawnee, and she took the rope from Edohi's hand.

"*Wado,*" she said.

"He calls himself the Outcast," said Edohi, "and he speaks our language."

"Come on then, Outcast," the Spoiler said, and she led him by the rope to her house.

The crowd was slowly dispersing, some individuals going first to Edohi to congratulate him. When most of them had gone their ways, Edohi looked toward his mother and her brother who were just standing there, just waiting. They moved together, and he walked to them.

"Uncle," he said, "you know why I've done this thing."

"Yes," said Hemp Carrier, "I know."

Wild Hemp smiled and nodded her head. "We know," she said.

"I want Corn Flower for my wife."

"We have already talked to her clan," said Hemp Carrier.

"Presents have been given," said Wild Hemp. "And we'll talk some more."

"Soon," said Edohi. It was not a demand, but neither was it a question.

"Very soon," said his mother.

Edohi looked around, but Corn Flower was no longer in sight. Perhaps it was just as well.

Like-a-Pumpkin was at the water. It was low, and it was dirty. It was well beyond the time, he thought, for these people to pack up and move their camp. Under ordinary, decent, human conditions, Like-a-Pumpkin would not even have considered using such water, not for bathing, certainly not for cooking or drinking. At the edge of the stream the water was especially dark, thick with stirred-up mud. Black and Red's woman stood behind Like-a-Pumpkin, a long stick in her hand. It was almost like a staff. It reminded Like-a-Pumpkin of the time which now seemed to him so long ago when he and his companions had begun their journey, robes covering their bodies, bundles tied on their backs, long staffs in hand.

He was at the abused stream with a water bag to fill. He wasn't sure, but he thought that the bag had been fashioned from a buffalo paunch. Like-a-Pumpkin had seen but few buffalo in his life, but he had heard that the shaggy beasts were larger in the west than were those who occasionally roamed through his eastern homeland. The woman had thrust the bag at him and prodded him with the stick toward the stream. Like-a-Pumpkin did not know where Black and Red might be, so there was no one but the woman to boss him around. He squatted there beside the water, his bare feet sinking in mud, and he looked at the murky water. Out in the middle of the stream, the water was not quite so bad as was that at the edge. He straightened up and waded into the water. It was not cool. He moved slowly, trying not to stir the mud. At its deepest point, the water almost reached his knees. He eased the water bag into the stream trying to skim clean water off the top. It was not clean. It was less dirty.

Then Like-a-Pumpkin sat down in the water. It was the first time since his captivity he had given in to a sudden urge to do something for his own comfort and pleasure. He felt bold and a little foolish. He splashed water over his upper body and onto his face and head. The woman said something that sounded like a question. Like-a-Pumpkin looked at her and smiled.

"I'm trying to wash off some of the filth from your nasty camp," he said. He knew that she couldn't understand his words. He wouldn't have said them if she could. Still it gave him a certain amount of pleasure to say them. He splashed more warm, dirty water over his head, his grin still wide. He noticed that some of the other people had come down to the stream, it seemed, just to watch. He looked from one to another, smiling.

"Is it so unusual among you to see a man bathe?" he said. "Yes. I'm sure that it is."

Black and Red's woman barked something at him and gestured. She was telling him to get out of there. He wasn't going to push his luck. He stood up and waded back out carrying the water bag. She said something more and reached out and took the bag from him. That puzzled him. Why would she take the heavy bag and carry it all the way back to her hovel? She held the water bag in one hand and with the other she pointed the staff at him, placing its end against his sternum. She pushed, and Like-a-Pumpkin fell over, landing on his back in the stream, making a large splash. The few people who had gathered laughed heartily, pointing at him, naked, flailing in the muddy water. He stood up and laughed with them. Black and Red's woman was already walking away from the stream. He raced after her like a faithful dog and took the water bag from her to lug it back to the tent.

Seventeen

STANDING-IN-THE-DOORWAY had also gone to the water, and the water he had gone to was also low, but unlike the murky water in which poor Like-a-Pumpkin wallowed, the waters of the Tanasi were still cool, still clear. Standing-in-the-Doorway was alone. At the water's edge he paused. He stood quiet and alert, listening for the voice of Long Man, trying to catch words, meaning, out of the elusive sounds of the passing waters. At last giving up, frustrated, he disrobed, and, standing naked there beside the waters, he prayed.

He prayed to Long Man, begging for understandable words of wisdom. Looking up, he prayed to the sun, begging for mercy, pleading with her to take pity on the suffering earth and the creatures who lived on the earth, reminding her that her intense rays could be deathly to mortal beings. He called on Thunder, reminding him of his promised friendship to the Real People.

"Send my three priests back home to me," he prayed, "and send clouds and rain along with them."

He prayed, but he received no answer. He saw no sign. The air, heavy with heat, weighed down upon his soul. The sun's rays burned his skin. The bright sky caused him to squint his eyes. And impure thoughts invaded his mind when it should have been concentrating on prayer. He thought about the smooth skin and the soft flesh of Two Heads. He longed for the full lips and the wet tongue. He sighed a heavy sigh and squatted beside the clothing and accessories he had put aside. There was but one thing left for him to do.

He picked up the stick that was lying there where he had left it on top of his cloak. It was as long as the distance between his elbow and the tip of his index finger. A piece of an ash branch, it was a straight and smooth wand, its bark carefully peeled. He took it with him, and he waded into the river. The body which had been suffering from the dry heat was shocked by the cold waters of Long Man, but Standing-in-the-Doorway waded on until water reached above his lower ribs. He stood there, and he put one end of the stick into his mouth, allowing it to gather his saliva. Taking it out of his mouth, he put the other end into the water, and he began to stir with wide circular motions.

He stirred until he had created a small eddy. Then he stopped, and he stared intently into its core. He held his breath. He did not blink. His heart pounded obtrusively in his chest. He waited for the eddy to fade, watching, hoping to see—nothing, nothing but water. Barely a wide, circular ripple was left, and Standing-in-the-Doorway dared to draw some air into his lungs. Somewhat relieved, he was about to turn to leave the water when a dried and twisted oak leaf floated by, slicing the barely perceptible circle in half.

"Ah," he said, and that was all he said, for he had just seen the sign of death.

The Spoiler tied the end of the rope that bound the Outcast to one of the upright poles which framed the doorway in the front of her house. Then she walked around to face him, and she laughed in his face.

"Ha. Now I have my own Shawnee dog," she said.

"Will you kill me?" he asked.

"Maybe," said the Spoiler. "Probably. But not real soon. When I get tired of you. First I want everyone to see you here, tied to my house. I want them all to know that your life is in my hands."

"I'm not afraid to die," said the Outcast. "I'm ready to die."

The Spoiler snorted and turned her back on her slave.

"It will be easy to kill you," she said. "I've killed Shawnees before, and they weren't tied up like you are here. No. I think I'll keep you alive for a while. I think I'll keep you for a slave. My Shawnee dog to fetch and carry."

"You've killed Shawnees? In war?"

"Yes. But not enough to make up for my man," she said. "Not enough."

"May I know your name?" asked the Outcast.

"Yes. All right," she said. "Why not? You should know. I am called the Spoiler."

"Ah," said the Outcast, his face registering surprise, even betraying a little admiration, "the Spoiler of the *Allegewis*. I've heard tales about you."

The Spoiler raised her eyebrows and smiled.

"Yes?" she said. "So the Shawnees remember me. Good. That's as it should be. Yes. Maybe I'll keep you alive for a good long while."

"I would rather be killed," he said.

"What you want is of no concern to me."

Just then some people came walking by. The Spoiler stopped them.

"Look. Look," she said. "Have you seen my Shawnee slave? My dog? Come and look at him. Edohi gave him to me. My dog."

It was late that evening when Wild Hemp showed up at the house of the Spoiler. The Outcast sat on the ground in front of the house. Wild Hemp glanced at him, then looked away.

"Spoiler," she said, "are you home?"

The Spoiler appeared in the doorway.

"Wild Hemp, my friend," she said. "Sit here with me."

She indicated a bench in front of her house. It was on the opposite side of the door from where the Outcast sat on the ground.

"Wait for me," said the Spoiler. "I'll get us something."

She went back inside to emerge a moment later with a clay bowl in her hands. She handed it to Wild Hemp and sat down beside her. Wild Hemp lifted the bowl to her lips and tipped it, taking a long and satisfying drink. The hominy corn drink was soured, the way Wild Hemp liked it best. She handed the bowl back to her host, and the Spoiler drank.

"*Wado*," said Wild Hemp. "That's good *gah-no-hey-nuh*."

"Your son has grown into a fine young man," said the Spoiler. She gestured casually toward the Outcast. "This was a fine thing he did for me."

"Yes," said Wild Hemp. "He's a good son. But you know, he really did it for himself."

The Spoiler handed the bowl back to Wild Hemp and gave her a knowing look and a nod.

"Um," she said. "Yes. I know. I think I know what he wants from me."

"Yes," said Wild Hemp.

"Yes," said the Spoiler. "Yes."

"Your daughter," said Wild Hemp. "Corn Flower."

There, she thought, it's been said straight out at last. Then she waited apprehensively for the Spoiler to respond, and she attempted to cover her apprehension by drinking deeply from the bowl again.

"Yes, well, I'll agree," said the Spoiler, "if Corn Flower wants Edohi. Gone-in-the-Water has looked at his crystal. He said it will be all right."

And Corn Flower did indeed want Edohi, for at that very moment, she slipped with him into the shadow of some trees in a secluded spot by the river's edge. Watching each other in silence, they undressed, and then they moved together to embrace. They held each other close and tight as they knelt, then leaned over to lie on their sides. It was new for both of them. It was the first time. With their hands, they explored each other's body. At last Edohi moved on top of her.

"I've wanted this for a long time," he said.

"And so have I, Edohi," Corn Flower whispered in his ear. "So have I."

Like-a-Pumpkin woke up as usual, with a kick to the rump by Black and Red. The fierce warrior had returned late the previous evening with three of his companions. They had returned from some unspecified place bringing back grisly trophies of war: fresh and bloody scalps, chopped-off fingers, sliced-off ears. The returning warriors had been bloody, but Like-a-Pumpkin had not been able to tell whether the blood was their own or that of their victims. The whole village had celebrated late into the night, singing, dancing, displaying the bloody trophies. Men, women and children danced. To the ears of Like-a-Pumpkin, the songs were annoying noise, not much more than shrieking and harsh, hoarse shouts. And the dancing, he thought, was mere jumping, stomping and convulsive twitching. But he had been left alone.

Now, following Black and Red's rude kick, he rolled over and struggled to his knees, then got up to his feet. Black and Red put a hand on his shoulder and gave him a shove, turning him around so that Like-a-Pumpkin stood with his back to his master. Then Black and Red untied his hands. He slapped his shoulder to get his attention, nudged the ashes on the ground with the toe of his moccasined foot, then pointed toward the woods across the clearing. He could have dispensed with the whole routine. He could simply have kicked Like-a-Pumpkin and untied him, for Like-a-Pumpkin well knew what to do. It was the same routine each morning. He smiled his most ingratiating smile and bobbed his head up and down to show that he understood, then headed across the field singing a song. It was a rabbit song.

> *Tlage situhn galisgi sida ha.*
> *Ha nia li li. Ha nia li li.*

Black and Red followed him, casually, but he was carrying his bow and some arrows. Like-a-Pumpkin continued singing.

> On the edge of the field I dance about.
> *Ha nia li li. Ha nia li li.*

Like-a-Pumpkin began moving in rhythm to his own song as he sang. He looked around for a long time but managed to collect only a few small sticks. Then, still singing, beginning to dance, carefully watching the reaction of Black and Red, he reached into the woods for a stick. He was careful to keep one foot in the clearing and to stretch to get the stick.

"On the edge of the field," he sang. He did this stretching into the woods for a while before he decided to dance with both feet into the woods.

"*Ha nia li li,*" he sang as he danced. He picked up some sticks and moved back into the clearing, dropping the sticks into a pile.

On the edge of the field I dance about.

Again he went into the woods. Again he brought his sticks to the clearing and dropped them on the pile. He sang the song and danced by the pile of sticks. Then he went back into the woods. He spotted a nice, large, fallen branch several paces deeper into the trees. He looked out toward Black and Red, stopped singing and called out.

"Hey. Hey, ugly-face," he said, and he pointed toward the desirable branch. "Can I go get that one? Can I go that far? You won't shoot me, will you, nastiness?"

Black and Red looked in the direction Like-a-Pumpkin was pointing. He furrowed his brow in a quizzical look. Like-a-Pumpkin kept pointing.

"That one?" he said. "To beat you with? To poke up your nasty rear end?"

Black and Red stepped into the woods, still looking after Like-a-Pumpkin's pointing arm, and he saw the branch. The puzzled look left his face, and he said something and waved his arm, telling Like-a-Pumpkin to go ahead and fetch the branch. Like-a-Pumpkin danced out to it, resuming his rabbit song.

Tlage situhn galisgi sida ha.

He tried to lift the branch, but it was too long. It was awkward to handle. He broke a piece off of the smaller end and dropped it to the ground. He danced a few steps backward, then danced back up to the branch.

. . . I dance about.

He broke a second piece and dropped it. The branch was getting thicker. He pulled at it, and when it broke, he fell over on his back. Black and Red roared with laughter. Like-a-Pumpkin stood up, laughed at himself, and started to sing again as he went back to the branch. He pulled until he broke off another piece. Then he groaned out loud and dropped to his knees, his head hanging down. He was looking at a large rock on the ground beneath the branch.

Black and Red walked toward Like-a-Pumpkin. He moved slowly, and the puzzled look was back on his face. Like-a-Pumpkin was rocking back and forth on his knees, holding his stomach and singing low.

Ha nia li li. Ha nia li li.

Black and Red moved closer. He said something sharply to Like-a-Pumpkin, but Like-a-Pumpkin just continued rocking, rocking and singing.

Ha nia li li. Ha nia li li.

Black and Red stopped just behind Like-a-Pumpkin. He spoke again, and what he said had the sound of a question. Like-a-Pumpkin didn't answer. He rocked, and he sang.

   . . . li li. Ha nia li li.

Black and Red leaned down close to Like-a-Pumpkin and spoke again. Still he got no reaction. Still the rocking, the singing.

   . . . li li.

He put a hand on Like-a-Pumpkin's back and gave him a shove, the kind of shove one might give a sleeping man in an attempt to wake him up.

Suddenly Like-a-Pumpkin turned, and he swung his arm. His fist was clutching the big rock, and Black and Red saw it coming, but he couldn't react in time. He saw it coming, and he opened his mouth, but before any sound could come out, the big rock had smashed his nose and his lips to pulp, had blackened his eyes and broken all of his front teeth. He staggered back. He was blind with rage and pain, and he was blind because his eyes were caked with blood. His hands went to his face, and his face felt to him like a fresh cut of meat. He tried to shout, but his mouth was swollen, and it was mush, and he could make no noise. He was blind, and he was mute, and he was helpless.

Like-a-Pumpkin stood up and faced Black and Red. He looked with horror at what he had done. He turned as if to run, hesitated, then turned back to face Black and Red once again. He shot a glance toward the camp, but he could hear or see nothing to indicate that anyone back there suspected anything. He lifted the rock up to deal a final blow to the head of Black and Red, but he paused. Would a second blow finish off the man? Would it take several? Would he have to bash the head into mush? He didn't know. He dropped the rock, stepped in close to Black and Red, reached out and took the knife that was hanging at Black and Red's waist. With both hands gripping the hilt, he drove it upward with all his might, driving the rough but sharp-edged flint blade under the rib cage, up, and into the heart. Hot blood ran out onto his hands, and the body of Black and Red slumped forward, falling against Like-a-Pumpkin. Like-a-Pumpkin gave it a shove, and it fell away to land on its back on the ground. Like-a-Pumpkin looked around. Still no one was coming. He sang his song.

. . . *li li.*

He stripped the breechclout off the body and put it on himself. Then he took the moccasins and put them on his own feet. They were too big, but they would have to do. He took the bloody knife, and he took the bow and the four arrows that Black and Red had carried with him to the woods. He straightened up, and he spat on the bloody face of his fallen foe.

Ha nia li li. Ha nia li li.

He sang as he danced through the woods, moving farther and farther away from the hated village, watching over his shoulder as he danced away.

. . . *li li. . . . li.*

Edohi had gone out to hunt. His mother had returned from her meeting with the Spoiler and told him that the Spoiler had agreed. Edohi had then asked Corn Flower. That had, of course, been a formality. He had known that she would agree, and she did. Corn Flower went back to her mother, and then the Spoiler had made the announcement. Her daughter would marry Edohi in seven days. He had to kill a deer, and so he had gone out again. On his way out of town, he had passed the house of the Spoiler, and she had been outside standing beside her house at her *kanona*, the wooden beater made by scooping out a bowl shape in the top of a section of tree trunk. With a long pole she was pounding corn in the *kanona*. Edohi had avoided looking at her, and she did not speak, for it was forbidden for a man to speak to his wife's mother, or she to him. Edohi was not yet married, but everyone was agreed. He wasn't sure what to do, so he pretended not to see the Spoiler.

The Outcast was there, though, still tied to the house, sitting on the ground.

" '*Siyo*, Edohi," he said. "Now I know why you refused to kill me and why you brought me here. I don't blame you for what you did. She is a beautiful young woman, as beautiful almost as her mother."

The Spoiler had paused in her work long enough to eavesdrop, then she had resumed her pounding, harder and faster than before. Edohi couldn't think of an appropriate response to what the Outcast had said, so he just nodded his head and went on his way. He had to kill a deer.

Others had more work to do. The women of Corn Flower's clan would build a house for Corn Flower close to the Spoiler's house. It would belong to Corn Flower, and Edohi would live there with her. The Spoiler would also be busy making Corn Flower new moccasins and a new dress, and she would have help from other women in the clan. Edohi's mother, too, was making new clothes for her son. Edohi had the least to do. He had to kill a deer.

Corn Flower sat alone in the woods. She sat beneath a giant walnut tree taking advantage of its shade, and she leaned back against its thick, old trunk. From somewhere in the distance came the sound of the rapid tapping of a woodpecker, and all around her hidden bugs sang their songs. Corn Flower thought for a moment. Then she began to sing, softly, sending the new words up toward the heavens, not forcefully, easy, letting them float softly to find their own way.

> My lover has gone to hunt.
> *Ha wa la.*
> He's gone to kill a deer.
> *Ha wa la.*
> But he'll come back to me.
> *Ha wa la.*
> *Ha wa la wu.*
> I'm beautiful in his eyes.
> *Ha wa la.*
> In his eyes are no other women.
> *Ha wa la.*
> And now he's coming back to me.
> *Ha wa la wu.*

Edohi did not want to return to town until the seventh day, the day of his wedding, so he passed up several chances to kill deer. He would wait, he decided, until early morning of the seventh day, so the kill would still be fresh when he took it in. He knew he was being bold. He was taking a chance. What if he let all these chances go by, and then on the morning of the seventh day, he saw no deer? The thought crossed his mind, but it did not worry him. Edohi was a confident hunter, and there were plenty of deer. With smaller streams drying up, the animals were staying near the river. The lack of rain made it even easier than usual to locate deer. He stayed in the woods alone along the river, and he thought. He thought about what the wedding day would mean to his life. He thought about the past and his carefree childhood, now gone forever. He thought about the many long days he had spent playing in the woods with Corn Flower and Acorn. Acorn. Two Heads. What a thing he had become. He drove the distasteful image out of his mind, and he thought of Corn Flower and of her beauty, and he thought, what a thing *she* had become, and he thought about his approaching wedding day.

Early in the morning of the seventh day, he was waiting in the browsing field near Ijodi. He was waiting for his deer. And he didn't have to wait long. Four deer appeared. One was a healthy buck. Edohi waited for a clear shot. He nocked an arrow, aimed it and muttered a prayer for its true flight. Then on the last syllable of the prayer, he released the arrow. It struck its mark. The buck looked startled, tried to leap forward, then fell. The other three animals turned and fled into the woods. Edohi drew out his knife and ran toward his kill. Kneeling beside the body of the buck, he said a prayer to Awi-Usdi, Little Deer, the spirit chief of all the deer. It was a prayer of thanks, and it was an apology.

He cut its throat, and he gutted it. He ate the liver raw, bloody and still warm. Then he tied its feet together, slung it over his shoulders and headed for Ijodi.

Two Heads was there, but he stayed back, lurking in the shadows, not talking to anyone, not taking part in the festivities. He was a distant onlooker, not a participant. If any noticed him there, they paid him no heed. There was a big feast, but otherwise there was little ceremony. The men had all been fed. Women and children were eating. Over by the *gatayusti* field a group of men had cornered Edohi.

"So this is your big day," said one of the men.

"I bet something else will be big soon," said another.

Edohi grinned and ducked his head as the others all laughed.

"When she takes you to her new house," someone said, "will you know what to do?"

"Oh," said another, "maybe he's already done it."

They laughed some more, and now and then Edohi received good-natured shoves. He would be glad when this was all over and done.

Inside the townhouse women had Corn Flower surrounded.

"I don't think she knows what she's in for," said a young married woman. "This Edohi never stays home."

"That's good," said an older one. "I wish I could make my man stay away from home so long."

The women all laughed, and Corn Flower smiled politely.

"I hope you'll know what to do tonight," said another older woman. "Have you had plenty of practice? I hope you have. Your fun years are all over now. Now you have to settle down and be faithful to just one man."

"Edohi is all the man I'll ever want," said Corn Flower.

"Ah," shouted the old woman, "she *has* already tried him out."

All of the women roared with laughter.

The people all gathered around the plaza to watch. For such an important occasion, one that had been preceded with such elaborate and careful preparation, the ceremony itself was brief, simple, to the point, even plain. Edohi and Corn Flower walked out to the center of the plaza facing each other. Edohi held out for her a choice cut of the deer he had killed that very morning. It signified to her, to her clan and to all the witnesses present that he was able to provide for her by hunting. She took the venison, symbolically taking Edohi, and she offered him an ear of corn. He accepted. Then old Gone-in-the-Water stepped out of the crowd carrying a buffalo robe. As he held it out wide open before him, Edohi and Corn Flower stood close together, and the conjurer wrapped the single robe around them both. Then, huddled together inside the robe, they walked to Corn Flower's house, the new house built for her by her clan, and they were man and wife.

Standing-in-the-Doorway stood alone on the temple mound at Men's Town staring at the western sky. It was clear. The air was hot and dry. He thought about the three priests he had sent on the mission to the west, and he wondered where they might be, how near to their destination, how much longer before their return. When would the rains come? And he thought about Two Heads and wished that the young man would hurry back from Ijodi. It was getting late. He had much on his mind, and he did not want to be alone. He suddenly felt a powerful sadness settle over him like a dark pall, and in spite of the heat, it gave him a chill. It was like the end of day approaching, except it was bigger, darker and more mysterious. And then he thought about the leaf in the eddy.

Inside Corn Flower's new house, the house where he would live, Edohi stood gazing in awe at the beauty of his wife. His wife. Life was a great mystery. This beautiful woman standing before him, his wife, had been, just yesterday it seemed, a girl he ran and played with in the woods, had been, in fact, just like another boy to him. And now, he thought, and now— He felt like dropping to his knees in front of her and offering prayers of thanks. He felt like he should be making new songs, songs of love and praise, and singing them out loud for all of Ijodi to hear.

"I guess I should go to my mother's house," he said, "and get my things."

"Tomorrow will be time enough for that," said Corn Flower, and she pulled her new, soft, doeskin dress off over her head and stood before him wearing—nothing at all. She reached for him and pulled him down with her to the thick, soft cushion of the buffalo robe there on the floor, and soon nothing else mattered, not the priests, not even Two Heads, not the terrible heat and its companion drought, for Edohi was lost in her love.

Author's Note

The Way of the Priests and the novels which are planned to follow it were suggested to me by a tale from the Cherokee oral tradition which was collected in the 1890s on the Cherokee reservation in North Carolina by James Mooney and published in *Myths of the Cherokees* by the Bureau of American Ethnology in its 19th Annual Report as "The Massacre of the Ani-Kutani." (Many of the old tales retold here also appeared in that report.)

The story as I imagine it takes place shortly before the arrival of Europeans in America. The setting is in what is now the southeastern United States. The old Cherokee country covered all or parts of present-day North Carolina, South Carolina, Tennessee, Kentucky, West Virginia, Georgia and Alabama. This book begins what is projected as an ongoing series which will trace Cherokee history through fiction.

There are advantages to that approach. For example, I have included among the priests a scribe, assuming that the Cherokee syllabary, supposed to have been invented in the early nineteenth century by Sequoyah, was actually an ancient writing system. That, of course, flies in the face of the widely held belief that all American Indian societies were preliterate before the arrival of Europeans. But I believe that the Cherokee syllabary *may* be an old system, and therefore it exists in *The Way of the Priests*. (I am not, by the way, the first to make this claim. Traveller Bird, a Cherokee, did so earlier in a book about Sequoyah called *Tell Them They Lie.)*

Work on the Cherokees by many other writers has enriched my own knowledge over the years and has therefore contributed to my own current efforts, but I would like to here acknowledge other valuable sources: people I have spent hours talking with over the years about all kinds of things Cherokee: history, culture, art, religion, language. My sincere thanks then to Wilma P. Mankiller, Principal Chief of the Cherokee Nation; Dr. Charles Gourd; Dr. Charles Van Tuyl; the late Wesley Proctor and his sister Adalene Proctor Smith; Earnie Frost; artists Murv Jacob, Jane Osti, Bob Annesley and Cecil Dick; Tommy Belt; Dr. Willard Walker, anthropologist and linguist; and finally my main critic and source of inspiration, my wife, Evelyn Snell Conley (Guwisti Elaqui).

Glossary

Cherokee words, phrases and names from *The Way of the Priests*

Agehyuja girl.

Agili He-Is-Rising, a masculine name.

Anagalisgi Lightning, mythic third son of Thunder.

Aneja the ball play, or ball game, sometimes called "the little brother of war," similar to lacrosse.

Ani a plural prefix, often translated as "people."

Ani-Chahta Choctaws, or Choctaw People.

Ani-chuja boys, also used to designate the mythic sons of Thunder, also called "the Thunder Boys," "the Little Thunders" and "the Little Men."

Ani-Kawi *ani + awi*; the "k" is present to avoid a hiatus. Deer People, one of the seven Cherokee clans.

Ani-Kituwah Kituwah People (see *Kituwah*).

Ani-Kutani the ancient priesthood of the Cherokees (see *Kutani*).

Ani-nuhdawegi Iroquois People.

Ani-Sakonige Blue People, one of the seven Cherokee clans.

Ani-Sawahani Shawnee People.

Ani-Senika Seneca People.

Anisgaya *ani + asgaya*. Men.

Anisgaya-Tsunsdiga Little Men, Little Thunders, the Thunder Boys.

Anisgayayi Men's Town. The suffix *yi* indicates "place of" or "place for."

Ani-Skalali Tuscarora People.

Ani-Tsiksu Chickasaw People.

Ani-Tsisqua Bird People, one of the Cherokee clans.

Ani-yunwi-ya the Real People. *Ani* + *yunwi* (person) + *ya* (real or original). Originally, the Cherokees' name for themselves.

Aquanuhgis the Delawares or Lenni-Lenape.

Asgaya man.

Asgaya Gigagei Red Man, a ceremonial name for Thunder.

Astugataga Standing-in-the-Doorway, a masculine name.

Awi deer.

Awi-Usdi Little Deer, the mythic spirit chief of the deer.

Ayasta the Spoiler, a feminine name.

Dagunahi Mussel Shell Place, an ancient Cherokee town.

Dahlonega the color yellow, also the name of an ancient Cherokee town, so named, perhaps, because of gold fields nearby, located in what is now Georgia.

Dakwa a large mythical fish. The word is also used to indicate a whale.

Dalala the red-bellied woodpecker.

Da-le-danigisgi Hemp Carrier, a masculine name.

Dasuntali Stinging Ant, a masculine name.

Dayunisi Beaver's Grandchild, a water beetle prominent in the Cherokee origin story.

Edohi He-Is-Going-About, or He-Is-Walking, a masculine name.

Etawa Tsistatlaski Deadwood Lighter, a masculine name.

Gah-no-hey-nuh a drink made of hominy corn. It can be served cold or hot. Traditionally served to visitors.

Gatayusti a gambling game of ancient origin played with a stone disc or wheel and a throwing arrow or spear.

Gatuhnlati Wild Hemp, a feminine name.

Guhna wild turkey.

Gule acorn.

Ha nia li li vocables, comparable to "tra la la" in modern English song lyrics.

Ha wa la wu vocables.

Hlesdi stop, quit it.

Howa okay, all right.

Ijodi common, current spelling, *Echota*. The name of an ancient Cherokee town. The meaning of the word is lost.

Iya-Iyusdi *iya* (pumpkin) + *iyusdi* (like). Pumpkin-Like, or Like-a-Pumpkin, a masculine name.

Jisdu rabbit, also spelled Tsisdu or Chisdu. Rabbit is the Trickster of Cherokee and other southeastern American Indian myth.

Kanati mythic hero, husband of Selu, associated with Thunder, known as "the Great Hunter." Meaning of name is lost.

Kanegwati Water Moccasin (the snake), a masculine name.

Kanona a beater, a section of log or tree trunk with the top end scooped out to form a bowl shape, used with a long pole as a beater, like a large mortar and pestle.

Kituwah also spelled Keetoowah, the name of an ancient Cherokee town, known as a "mother town." Sometimes thought of as the original town. Hence Cherokees also refer to themselves as Kituwah People *(Ani-Kituwah)*. The meaning of the word is lost.

Kutani a priest, exact meaning lost.

Ni   look, look here, hey.

Nikutsegi   the name of an ancient Cherokee town, meaning lost. Later forms of the word are Nickajack and Nigger Jack.

Osi   the hot house, sweat house or winter house. A small house beside the main dwelling.

Osiyo   a greeting.

Sakonige   the color blue.

Saloli   squirrel.

Sawahani   a Shawnee.

Selu   corn. Also the name of the wife of Kanati and the mythic Corn Mother.

Selu Ajiluhsgi   Corn Flower, a feminine name.

Senika   a Seneca.

'Siyo   common contracted form of *osiyo*.

Sudagi   name of a creek near Ijodi. Meaning of name is lost.

Suli   buzzard.

Tanasi   the name of a river. Meaning is lost but contemporary form is "Tennessee."

Tlage situhn galisgi sida ha   On the edge of the field I dance about. Lyrics to the rabbit's song from the story of Rabbit's escape from the wolves, recorded by James Mooney in *Myths of the Cherokee*.

Tlanuwa   mythical giant hawk. Translation lost.

Tsiksu   a Chickasaw.

Tsisqua   bird.

Tsisquaya   real bird, the sparrow; *tsisqua* (bird) + *ya* (real or original). Also a masculine name.

Tsusginai   Ghost Place or Ghost Country. The place on the other side of the mythic Sky Vault where the souls of the dead reside.

Tunai   masculine name, meaning lost.

Ujonati   rattlesnake.

Ukitena Keen-Eyed, a mythic, anomalous monster. Often contracted to *uk'ten'*.

Uluhnsadi transparent, divining crystal, said to be obtained from the forehead of the *uk'ten'*.

Untsaiyi onomatopoeic name of the mythical, shapechanging Gambler. The word imitates the sound of something striking a sheet of metal (like the English "ping"). In modern times translated as "Brass."

Usunhiyi the Darkening Land, where it is always twilight, where the souls of the dead go, and where some supernatural beings live. It's to the west on the other side of the Sky Vault.

Wado thank you.

Yansa buffalo or bison. In their early days, the Cherokees and other eastern Indians were acquainted with the eastern woodland bison, a larger and more timid animal than its plains cousin.

Yona Equa Big Bear, a masculine name. Yona (bear) + *equa* (big).

Yunwi Ganahida *yunwi* (person) + *ganahida* (long). Long Person, a ritual name for the river, personified and spiritualized. Long Person is a giver of life and of long life. He also speaks to those who know how to listen.

Non-Cherokee Words

Allegewi Shawnee and Delaware name for the Cherokees. Meaning may be "Cave Dwellers." Contemporary form—Allegheny.

Chalakee Choctaw name for Cherokees. Meaning may be "Cave Dwellers." Europeans picked up the word from the Choctaws, and it evolved into the contemporary "Cherokee."

ABOUT THE AUTHOR

Robert J. Conley is a Western writer and editor who specializes in Cherokee lore. He is the author of four previous Double D Westerns, *Nickajack*, *The Saga of Henry Starr*, *Back to Malachi* and *The Actor*, and received a Spur Award from the Western Writers of America for his 1987 short story "Yellow Bird." He lives in Tahlequah, Oklahoma.

ABOUT THE ILLUSTRATOR

Painter/pipemaker Murv Jacob, a descendant of the Kentucky Cherokees, lives and works in Tahlequah, Oklahoma. His meticulously researched, brightly colored, intricate work centers on the traditional Southeastern Indian cultures and has won numerous awards.